"Why do you think I've come back here, Holly?"

She had started to shake inside. She felt sick with anger and distrust. Was Robert really trying to pretend that he had come back because he regretted the way he had hurt her, the way he had left her?

"I really don't know," she told him tightly, "and neither do I care. As far as I'm concerned the past is over...dead...finished."

PENNY JORDAN was constantly in trouble in school because of her inability to stop daydreaming—especially during French lessons. In her teens, she was an avid romance reader, although it didn't occur to her to try writing one herself until she was older. "My first half-dozen attempts ended up ingloriously," she remembers, "but I persevered, and one manuscript was finished." She plucked up the courage to send it to a publisher, convinced her book would be rejected. It wasn't, and the rest is history! Penny is married and lives in Cheshire.

Penny Jordan's striking mainstream novel *Power Play* quickly became a *New York Times* bestseller. She followed that success with *Silver, The Hidden Years, Lingering Shadows* and *For Better For Worse*.

Don't miss Penny's latest blockbuster, *Cruel Legacy,* available late 1995. "Women everywhere will find pieces of themselves in Jordan's characters."
—*Publishers Weekly*

Books by Penny Jordan

HARLEQUIN PRESENTS
1599—STRANGER FROM THE PAST
1625—MISTAKEN ADVERSARY
1655—PAST PASSION
1673—LESSON TO LEARN
1705—LAW OF ATTRACTION
1719—A MATTER OF TRUST
1738—TUG OF LOVE
1746—PASSIONATE POSSESSION

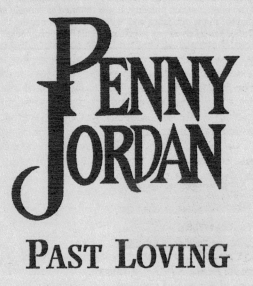

PENNY JORDAN

PAST LOVING

Harlequin Books

TORONTO • NEW YORK • LONDON
AMSTERDAM • PARIS • SYDNEY • HAMBURG
STOCKHOLM • ATHENS • TOKYO • MILAN
MADRID • WARSAW • BUDAPEST • AUCKLAND

ISBN 0-373-11756-6

PAST LOVING

First North American Publication 1995.

CHAPTER ONE

'AND then he said that he had to work late again; that's the third time in a fortnight. I know how much of his time your business is taking up now that it's expanding so much, Holly, and with all this media attention you've been getting, but honestly do I look like a fool? Working late...not on your accounts, I'll bet, and that new secretary of his had the gall to tell me that he was in a meeting when I rang him yesterday.'

Smoothing the neat straight skirt of her primrose yellow suit, Holly let Patsy's diatribe wash over her; not because she wasn't interested or didn't care about her old friend's problems—after all, instead of being here listening to Patsy complaining about Gerald, she had intended to spend her precious few hours helping Rory put in the tulips and forget-me-nots that were going to make such a lavish display of blue and yellow in the spring.

When Patsy had telephoned her, announcing that she had to see her because there was something she had to talk to her about, she had immediately assumed from the tragic tone of her friend's voice that something catastrophic had occurred.

Poor Gerald, the last thing he was likely to do was to be unfaithful to his volatile red-haired wife; Patsy was the one who had always had a rather elastic view of her marriage vows.

She tried to concentrate on what Patsy was saying and discovered that her friend had ceased complaining about Gerald's new secretary and was now complaining about the amount of work her own business was causing Gerald.

'I know Gerald himself would never mention it, but it isn't as though he's actually on your board or anything, is it? I mean, I know he's your accountant, but he does have other clients.'

Holly suppressed a grim smile. She ought to be used by now to the fact that some of her friends were inclined to be either envious or resentful of her unexpected commercial success. Many of them, like Patsy, also seemed to have a very inflated idea of her imagined new-found wealth. It was true that her company had become startlingly profitable, but the majority of those profits were being ploughed back into the business, the one luxury she had allowed herself being the purchase of the long low-built Tudor farmhouse several miles outside town.

Even as a girl she had loved Haddon's Farm, not quite as much as she had loved the Hall perhaps, but then what did one single woman want with a home that boasted over twenty bedrooms, a ballroom, and a drawing-room large enough to accommodate the entire downstairs of her own home, plus a library, two sitting-rooms, and a whole village of small dark and dank pantries and kitchens, even if she had been able to afford it?

No, the farm was much more her style... much more in keeping with the way she wanted to live. It had roots that went back almost as far as the village itself, pre-dating the Hall by almost a century, and best of all it had a wonderful range of outbuildings, even if they were half falling down and even if the gardens that surrounded the house had resembled a wilderness when she moved in.

All the more scope for her to implement her own ideas and desires, she had told Gerald and Paul mischievously when they had complained that she must be mad to take on such a time-consuming task, when by rights every bit of her time ought to be devoted to the business.

The business... The slim hand smoothing the yellow silk of her skirt went still.

Even now she found it hard sometimes to come to terms with the way the small business she had started at home in her father's garden shed had mushroomed into the high-profile success it was today.

Fresh from university, newly qualified as a chemist, she had found herself uneasy and unhappy with the modern emphasis on chemically produced beauty products. It had been the gift of a dog-eared Housekeeper's Receipt Book-cum-Herbal dating from the seventeenth century which had set her off along the alternative avenue of exploring the simpler, kinder methods of producing beauty products from natural sources which had eventually led to the successful business she had today. Things she had made initially just for herself or to test out the recipes in her herbal, their reputation initially spreading by word of mouth, loyally encouraged by Paul, her brother, who had entrepreneurially taken charge of the marketing side of her small business. She vividly remembered their début into the world of country fairs and market stalls. She had enjoyed those days, enjoyed that life, when she had been free to dress in a pair of tatty old jeans and a sweatshirt and to leave her hair free from the time-consuming restrictions of style and image.

Now things were different, especially over the last couple of years when she had been named 'New Businesswoman of the Year', and had somehow or other been swept up in a public-relations exercise which had now left her feeling uncomfortably at odds with herself, unfamiliar and sometimes very out of charity with the woman she saw in the mirror, a woman who had swapped her jeans for designer suits, a woman who no longer went bare-legged but who wore silk stockings, a woman whose silky fine hair had been skilfully cut and even more skilfully highlighted so that it fell in a soft blonde sheeny bob that emphasised the delicate purity of her skin and bone-structure...but most of all a woman who she was suddenly recognising *had* become a woman, and was no longer a girl.

She was thirty now...where on earth had the years gone? When she looked back to her late teens her life had worked out so differently from what she had imagined. Then she had expected and believed that she would marry, would have children, would be content and absorbed by the fulfilment of being the axis on which her husband's and her children's lives turned, just as her own mother had been, and yet here she was at thirty, not married, not a mother, but with the kind of high profile and successful career which she had so strenuously denied at eighteen was what she wanted. But then at eighteen she had believed herself to be in love; and what was more she had believed that that love was returned and that it was forever. How naïve she had been. These days, when she looked around at her friends' marriages and relationships, she was forced to realise just how idealistic her teenage dreams had been. Paul, her brother, was always complaining that she was too much of a daydreamer.

Paul. He was away in South America at the moment, gathering as much research material as he could from the tribes of the rain forests before their environment and the potentially irreplaceable properties of the things that grew there were lost forever, plants that could produce life-saving drugs, without the side-effects of synthetic products.

She moved restlessly on Patsy's chintz-covered settee, suddenly overwhelmed by the heavy scent of Patsy's perfume, the cloying over-stuffed prettiness of her carefully designed sitting-room. She ached to be outside in the fresh air, to be dressed in her oldest jeans, turning over spades full of soft loamy earth, feeling the excitement and pleasure of siting the bulbs, of allowing her imagination to paint for her the colourful picture they would make in the spring, in their uniform beds set among lawn pathways and bordered by a long deep border of old-fashioned perennial plants. The kitchen window overlooked those beds, and beyond them on the other side of the wall lay her herb and vegetable garden.

Robert had always teased her about her fascination with growing things, claiming that it must be a throwback...a resurgence of those genes which had led to her father's family producing generation after generation of farmers.

In her grandparents' day, though, farming had not been profitable enough to support a family and so the farm had been sold and her own father had qualified as an accountant, even though he had never been drawn to city life and had remained living in the village where he had been brought up.

Her brother had none of the need for roots and continuity that so motivated her; he was a traveller, a restless adventurer whose quicksilver brain never allowed him to rest. No wonder he and Robert had been such good friends. Had been ... Holly wondered if they were still in touch. Paul certainly never mentioned him much these days—or at least he hadn't mentioned him until recently...until his name and his photograph had begun to feature so prominently on the pages of the financial Press.

She could feel her muscles starting to tense, her mind and body preparing to reject the mental image she could feel trying to threaten her peace of mind. In vain she tried frantically to concentrate on the soothing mental spectacle of the frothy mass of deep blue forget-me-nots and the tall elegant blooms of golden yellow tulips, but instead, traitorously, the only image her brain cells would produce was one of a lithe dark-haired man, the image in her own memory-banks subtly altered to allow for the passage of time, so that the hardness of his bone-structure was more apparent, and the cool clarity of his blue-grey eyes reinforced by time and experience.

Robert had always known what he wanted from life, had always known where he was going; the pity of it was that she had misguidedly believed that she was a part of that life plan; that when he told her he loved her, he meant he would always love her.

Memories she didn't want to acknowledge started to surface: emotions, needs, feelings she had told herself over ten years ago that she had to suppress and destroy.

How many girls of eighteen or thereabouts suffered what she had suffered and walked away from that suffering without a backward glance? Why was it that she had never been able to say truthfully to herself that she was over Robert, that the memory of him no longer caused her the slightest surge of pain?

She had been careful with her relationships since then, careful to admit into her life men whom she knew could never threaten her emotional barriers, men whom she liked, whose company she enjoyed, men whom she knew would have liked to take their relationship a step further from that of good friends to that of lovers, men who in many cases and with only the slightest encouragement could easily have fallen in love with her and wanted to spend their life with her, but she had been too afraid to allow that ... afraid of making the wrong judgement ... afraid of allowing herself to love again, only to be rejected again. And what, after all, was she missing out on? Not the idealistic union of two people who were all in all to one another, lovers, friends, companions, mutually loving and supportive, intensely loyal, sufficient only to themselves, as she had imagined that marriage would be when she was in love with Robert.

No, when she looked at her friends' marriages, none of them was like that, although in the main most of them worked . . . after a fashion.

She knew so many women who said openly that their relationships with their husbands came a poor second to their love for their children and that it was that love that cemented their marriages together; and she also knew many men who claimed over business lunches and to her irritation and annoyance that their wives no longer cared for them, no longer put them first, no longer treated them with the adoration and worship they believed they deserved. And yet somehow or other their marriages kept going.

Perhaps the fault was hers in that she as an outsider looking in saw the flaws . . . or perhaps it was simply her mind's defence mechanism, a way of comforting her and of telling her that she was better off the way she was . . . better off staying single rather than risking the precarious waters of marriage, rather than allowing herself to risk the pain that went with love.

No, nothing in her life had worked out as she had planned. She glanced across at Patsy, who was still complaining about Gerald, her face twisted into prematurely aging lines of bitterness and irritation. Patsy, who during their teens had been the one who had said challengingly and determinedly that she was going to make something of her life, that she wasn't going to stay mouldering away in the country when there was all the excitement of the city waiting for anyone with the enterprise and will-power to take up that challenge.

And so what had Patsy done? She had taken herself off to London, and got herself a job working at a gallery off Bond Street, where she had promptly and foolishly had an affair with the owner, which had resulted in her summary dismissal when her boss's wife had found out, plus an unscheduled and very unpleasant visit to a private abortion clinic.

Patsy had told her all this in a tearful and wine-induced confession on the eve of her marriage to Gerald. Gerald, the childhood sweetheart she had come home to marry, when the glitter of city life had begun to pall. Gerald, who in Patsy's estimation was her consolation prize in life for failing to win something more enticing in its lottery.

And yet here was Pasty complaining that she thought that Gerald might be being unfaithful to her.

Automatically Holly started to reassure her, only to be interrupted when Patsy struck out venomously, 'Well, of course you would say that. Honestly, Holly, you've always got your head in the clouds. You never see reality. It's no wonder that you're still unmarried—which reminds me . . . Guess who's bought the Hall?'

Holly waited, her face calm and she hoped expressionless. She knew what was coming and had known it all weekend, in fact, since Rory, arriving with a load of manure for the roses, had casually announced that the Hall had been sold and guess who had bought it? He, of course, was a decade younger than her, far too young to have known, even less remembered that once she and Robert Graham had been 'going steady' or that she had assumed that their relationship was going to lead to an engagement and then to marriage. That she had already chosen the names of their first two children...that she had cosily envisaged the life they would lead together...that she had believed, when Robert said he loved her, that he meant the words...had believed that when they were lovers their physical union meant far, far more than the mere joining of their two bodies. Her mouth twisted a little self-mockingly, her eyes darkening with the memory of that gut-wrenching, shockingly acid pain she had felt the night Robert had told her that he was going to America to do a post-graduate degree in business studies...the night he had made it clear to her that she had simply been a brief diversion, a means of passing the long summer months before he went on with the real business of following his life plan. Where she had dreamed of forever, marriage, babies and everything that to her went with the commitment she had made to him, he had seen other and very different horizons.

He had stared at her in open disbelief when Holly had haltingly tried to express her feelings, shocked into protesting that he couldn't mean what he was saying by the intensity and immediacy of her raw disbelief that he could actually be doing this, that he could actually be telling her that he was leaving for Harvard at the end of the month and that their relationship was over.

'Marriage? But you're only eighteen. You're going to university in September. You're too young...'

You're too young. How neatly and logically he had used her youth against her, exonerating himself from all blame...from any guilt.

Where now she might have bitterly pointed out that she had also been too young for the sophisticated game of casual sex he had obviously been playing with her, then she had been too shocked, too hurt...too overwhelmed to remind him of those words of love he had whispered to her when he had held her in his arms, to remind him of the passionate intensity of their lovemaking...to remind him that at eighteen she had been too young and too unknowing to be able to differentiate between a man's desire for sex and a girl's infatuated desire for what she perceived to be love.

Now, with over a decade of experience separating her from the girl she had been then and the woman she was now, she waited patiently with a calmly serene face for Patsy to unload her burden of news, allowing only the merest flicker of response to cross her face when Patsy told her importantly, 'Robert Graham is back. I thought I'd better warn you...'

'Warn me?' Holly enquired politely, allowing her voice to express a faint puzzlement with her friend's intensity. 'Warn me about what?'

'Well...well, about the fact that he's back,' Patsy told her, floundering a little. 'I mean, I can re-

member how devastated you were when he dropped
you—well, we all can. I was saying to Lucy only
the other day that we all thought that you and
Robert would be married by the time you were
twenty-one . . .'

Grimly suppressing her real feelings, Holly allowed herself to appear relaxed and to smile. The
media-familiarisation course her PR adviser had
virtually forced her to go on was having some benefits after all, she decided with irony.

'Good heavens, Patsy, that was over ten years
ago. You don't surely still think that silly teenage
crush on Robert Graham has any bearing on my
life today, do you? Heavens, I can barely even remember what the man looks like. He must be well
into his thirties by now.'

She managed to make it sound as though Robert
were merely one step away from drawing his
pension, her smile and shrug implying that the
woman she was today could only derive amusement
and disdain at the thought of her childish folly in
loving such a man.

Patsy's mouth dropped open a little.

'You mean you aren't bothered?'

'About what?' Holly enquired, smoothing a non-
existent crease from her suit. The combination of
primrose yellow silk and her highlighted blonde hair
was one which she privately considered to be gilding
the lily, but her PR consultant had been insistent
that for the sake of the business she must present
an image with which other women could not only
identify, but which they could also aspire to.

'But it's not the real me,' she had protested, wrinkling her nose with distaste.

'It will be,' Elaine Harrison had told her robustly with a determined look. 'It will be.' And rather weakly she had given in, more because she felt that she owed it to everyone else, those who had supported her and the business in the early days when she was struggling to make ends meet, than because it was what she personally wanted.

'We aren't changing you,' Elaine had pointed out more kindly. 'Just emphasising certain aspects of you.'

No, they hadn't changed her. But sometimes she wished . . .

'About Robert moving back here,' Patsy was saying. 'I mean I thought he'd left for good. From what I've read in the papers he's so high-powered and everything now that I never thought he'd want to come back here to live. Every time you read about him, he seems to be jetting off to a different part of the world to see one of his clients. A management consultant…you'd think he'd live in New York or London.'

Her voice expressed her dissatisfaction that someone who could choose to live somewhere so glamorous would bury themselves in a quiet English village. Personally Holly couldn't think of anything worse than living in a large impersonal city…but then she was not Patsy. She wasn't Robert Graham either, and although she wasn't going to say as much she too was surprised that he should base himself here in the country.

Patsy was wrong about one thing, though... Far from jetting all over the world to see his clients, his eminence and reputation these days was such that they were the ones jetting in to see him—and he was no longer someone employed by millionaires. He was one himself.

Not that she envied him that. Large wealth brought with it its own set of very complex responsibilities, as she was beginning to discover.

'So you're not bothered about it, then?'

Patsy sounded quite disappointed. For the first time a glimmer of amusement broke through the icy apprehension which had frozen the normally warm core of her life since she had learned that Robert was coming back. No wonder she had turned to her garden for solace, desperately planning colour schemes for the spring, desperately giving herself something to hold on to, something to reach out for, something to look forward to once the long cold months of winter were over.

'I'm bothered about all manner of things,' she corrected Patsy with a faint smile. 'I'm bothered about the ecology, about the destruction of the rain forests, about the destruction we, the human race, are wreaking not just against one another but against our whole environment——'

'Oh, yes...I know about that,' Patsy interrupted pettishly. 'But that wasn't what I meant and you know it. I meant were you bothered about Robert coming back?'

Holly stood up. As she reached for her bag, the soft swing of her hair skilfully hid her face.

'No, I'm not. Why should I be?' she questioned, adding wryly, 'As I've just said, all manner of things do "bother me", as you put it, Patsy...things which are far, far more important to me than Robert Graham could ever be.'

She smiled at her friend as she straightened up and added dulcetly, 'And as for Gerald, I really don't think you need to worry. Have you actually met his new secretary yet?'

'No. No, I haven't, why?'

'She's fifty-five, married with two grown-up children and four grandchildren,' Holly told her drily.

Outside she stood in the sun for a while, enjoying its beneficent September warmth. Last night there had been a full moon, and the night air had been cool, a foretaste of the autumn to come. She thought about her wardrobe, bulging with the new autumn clothes the PR girl had almost forcibly made her buy. They were launching their new range of natural perfumes and body products before Christmas; there would be a rash of media interviews to attend. She had to look the part...and there were now so many things to consider. She herself had insisted that she would only wear clothes made in natural fibres, and then had been irritated when Elaine had solemnly pronounced, 'Very good—yes, that will really underline your commitment to the environment and to the new green mood sweeping the country.'

She had wanted to protest there and then that her decision had nothing to do with fitting into a

given mould, but Elaine had already passed on to
other issues, complimenting her on her decision not
to have her hair permed but to keep it natural and
straight.

She had ached to point out that the shockingly
expensive hairdresser who cut it once monthly and
the even more horrendously expensive lightening
procedure which involved a trip to London every
month could hardly be described as natural, but
what was the point? In actual fact she rather liked
the simple elegance of her new hairstyle now that
she had had time to grow accustomed to it. It was
much more suitable for a woman of thirty than her
previous unstyled long hair had been, but she hated
the way she sometimes felt that she was being forced
into a specific image, just as she disliked the current
'fashion' for promoting environment-conscious
awareness and products in a way that really only
paid lip-service to the ethics that lay behind them.

But then, as Paul had wisely pointed out to her,
the more people who bought her products, the more
people would become aware of how precious and
how vulnerable nature's resources were, and the
profits her business made were even now helping
to preserve those resources, to fight off the effect
of their destruction.

She smiled wryly to herself as she unlocked her
car. Environmentally speaking, she supposed she
ought to have owned a bicycle and not a car... She
did use lead-free petrol, however, even if Paul, who
was in charge of the fleet-purchasing of cars for the
company, had stunned her by presenting her with
the keys for this bright red convertible model of the

same car he had leased for the other company executives.

When she had protested that it was far too vibrant, and far too high-powered for her, he had grinned at her and said, 'OK, I'll send it back, shall I?' and they had both burst out laughing.

'You're a rat,' she had told him affectionately. 'You knew I wouldn't be able to resist it.'

'Well, someone has to bring you down from the lofty heights and remind you occasionally that you are human and subject to the same vices as the rest of us,' he had told her, and behind his teasing she had realised what he was trying to say to her. She had never deliberately tried to appear holier than thou, and that was the last way she wanted people to perceive her, and so, feeling rather chastened by his comment, she had allowed Elaine to sweep her off to London and equip her with the new wardrobe she would be wearing for the rash of interviews she would be forced to face in October.

As she drove away from Patsy's, she thought how lucky she was to be able to work in a country environment.

The business had expanded to such an extent now that they had their own purpose-built factory and office complex, on a small industrial site outside their local market town and close to the nearest motorway complex, and it was there that she headed for now.

She had a meeting this afternoon to discuss the packaging for a new make-up range they hoped to bring out in time for Christmas. She glanced at the dashboard clock and realised she had spent rather longer with Patsy than she had intended. There was a short cut she could take, a narrow dusty country lane which would cut a good few miles off her journey, even though, strictly speaking, it was a privately owned road.

She turned off on to it a mile away from Patsy's house. It had been a hot summer; the grass that grew either side of the lane was just beginning to die back, blackberries glistened on the hedgerows. The thought of her mother's blackberry and apple crumble made her mouth water, but she wasn't likely to taste one this autumn. Her parents had only just embarked on a world cruise, something her father had been promising her mother they would do once he had retired. Even though she now had her own home, she missed them. Like her, her mother was a keen gardener, and together they would have spent the autumn months poring over plant catalogues.

Her mind on her garden and the pleasure of the work that still lay ahead of her there, she drove down the lane, the land to either side of her obscured by the overgrown hedges, so overgrown that as she approached a particularly bad bend the branches actually scraped against the sides of her car. It was a blind bend, impossible to see round and the lane was only wide enough for one car, so to be confronted by the imposing black bonnet of a brand new and very large Mercedes saloon coming in the opposite direction made her reach automatically for the brake-pedal, her heart in her mouth, guilt and tension tightening her stomach muscles as she immediately recognised Robert Graham as the driver of the other car.

Guilt because she knew quite well that this lane was the private rear entrance to the Hall, continuing on past it to rejoin the main road on the other side of the village, and tension because... well, because Robert had stopped his car and was getting out.

Why on earth had she ever implied that a man of thirty-odd was a man well past his sexual prime? A tiny shiver of a sensation she did not want to recognise ricocheted down her spine as she sat virtually frozen in her own seat, staring at him as he walked towards her.

CHAPTER TWO

DISTURBINGLY Robert was dressed not as the image projected both by the financial Press and the sleek bulk of his expensive car suggested—in the immaculate formality of a business suit and shirt—but in jeans and a checked shirt worn under a soft leather blouson jacket, the clothes soft and well-worn, lacking the image-conscious stiffness of clothes conspicuously brand new and bought 'for the country'.

No, these were clothes he was used to wearing, familiar and chosen for comfort. And yet for all the casualness of his clothes there was about him a very strong aura of power and control, emphasised by the impatient, semi-hostile way he was approaching her car, his forehead creased in a frown as he called out curtly to her once he was within earshot.

'I'm sorry, but you must have missed your way. This is a private lane——'

He stopped speaking abruptly, his frown deepening as he stared into the car and then demanded incredulously, 'Holly?'

She forced herself to remember that she was thirty and not eighteen. Her face felt as stiff as wood but somehow she managed to get her lips to creak into a facsimile of a polite and distant smile.

'Hello, Robert——' she began, but before she could continue he interrupted her, demanding,

'Were you looking for me?'

Looking for him? Now she was thirty, the spell of his unexpected appearance broken as she stared at him with cool irritation, not unmixed with anger at his arrogance. Did he think she was still a silly little girl of eighteen, needlessly running after a man who no longer wanted her?

'No, I wasn't,' she told him. 'Actually I didn't realise you were here. I had heard that you'd bought the Hall, of course, but I'm afraid I was just using your lane to take a short cut back to the main road. Something I'll have to get used to not doing...'

It gave her a sharp sense of pleasure to be able to deny his assumption that she had been looking for him and even more to know that it was the truth.

'The Hall's been empty for so long——' she started to add, but he cut across her comment, telling her,

'Well, I intend to have gates placed at either end of the lane, which should deter future trespassers, although in your case you could always have planned your journey so that you didn't need to take a short cut. As it is, one of us is going to have to reverse.'

Meaning that *she* was going to have to reverse, Holly suspected as she deliberately refused to make any response to his comment about the gates. The Hall had been empty for so long that she wasn't the only person using the lane as a short cut, and, while she could understand that any new owner would want to maintain his privacy, she felt that

Robert's comment to her had been double-edged, a means of warning her that the lane wasn't the only thing that was out of bounds as far as she was concerned.

Was he really so arrogant as to imagine that she still cherished the idealistic and stupid daydreams she had held at eighteen? Or was she simply being over-sensitive, over-reacting because of what Patsy had said earlier and because of the shock of seeing him so unexpectedly, of realising that, no matter how many times she had seen his photograph in the papers, it had not prepared her for the reality of him, for the sheer maleness of him, and for all the ways in which her stupefied senses were being bombarded by their awareness of him?

All right, so he was still one hell of a sensually attractive man, she fumed inwardly, and, all right, so a part of her was dismayingly vulnerable to that sensuality, but it was surely a vulnerability which was being heightened by shock—a vulnerability she would soon have under control?

After all, nothing was as great a deterrent to the headiness of physical excitement and awareness as the dulling mundaneness of proximity.

'I'd better be the one to reverse,' she heard Robert saying to her. 'After all, we're closer to the house than we are to the main road.'

She focused on him, automatically starting to thank him, but he was already turning away from her.

He reversed the large Mercedes with a smooth dexterity which she envied.

For a birthday present last year, Paul had booked her on to an advanced driving course, and, while she felt she had learned a good deal from it, she had finished it feeling inwardly that she lacked many of the assets needed to make a truly good advanced driver. Her worst fault, she knew, was that she was inclined to daydream while at the wheel ... as she had been doing just now.

The lane ran outside the main wall of the Hall and gates from the stable yard opened on to it. For the last few years they had remained closed, rotting slowly away, as the Hall remained empty, but today they stood open, and as Robert reversed through them into the stable yard she found herself slowing down so that she could peer curiously towards the house.

It was a long time since she had last been inside it—an unauthorised visit during a village fête held in its grounds when she had been much younger. Then she had been awed and amazed by the size of the rooms, wondering what on earth one very old lady would want with so many. She must have been eight or nine at the time. Paul, of course, had been the instigator of that piece of naughtiness. Robert had gone with them as well and it had been Robert who had rescued her, when she discovered that her legs were too short to make it over the open window-sill through which they had made their illegal entry into the house.

It had been from the secure haven of his arms that she had faced the irritation of Mrs Powers' housekeeper, who had demanded to know just what they were up to, and it had been Robert who had apologised and smoothed over her anger. She ought to have realised then that a male with such a powerful ability to refocus female emotions would never be content to marry early and settle for a placid domestic life.

After that incident she had worshipped Robert, but since Paul had bluntly told her that neither he nor Robert wanted her interfering in their games she had docilely restrained herself to worshipping him in silence and solitude.

Suddenly realising the construction which Robert might put on the fact that she was virtually sitting still with her car engine idling, she was just about to drive away when he got out of his own car and came towards her.

An absurd flood of self-consciousness made her duck her head, conscious of the burning heat searing her pale skin. She was blushing—something she had believed she had stopped doing a decade ago. She prayed that the soft swing of her hair would conceal her heightened colour from Robert, quickly starting to change gear as she prepared to drive off, but he had now reached her car and had placed a restraining hand on her own window.

'I had hoped to see Paul, but I understand he's away on business...'

'Yes,' she agreed tersely.

'Never mind, I'll have plenty of time to catch up with him once he gets back. When *will* he be back, by the way?'

'I'm not quite sure.'

'Mm ... well, I'm renting a small cottage locally while I oversee the renovation of this place, so I'm going to be around for the foreseeable future.'

He was leaning on the window as he spoke to her. She could smell the leather of his jacket, the soap tang of his skin. His hands were tanned, the nails clean and trimmed, but not manicured. There was a graze across the back of his hand and a small cut on one finger. She wondered how they had got there ... perhaps in defending one of the lovely women he always seemed to be photographed with from the attentions of the paparazzi? She switched her glance from his hand to her own. Hers too bore the odd scratch. She had been attacked by an over-vigorous climbing rose at the weekend, angrily defending its right to spread itself just as far and fast as it chose. The rose had definitely been the victor of that battle, but she had warned it of stiff pruning to come in the autumn if it insisted on its greedy absorption of territory that was not its to appropriate ...

In a garden, order had to be imposed if havoc was not to result.

'I'll let Paul know that you're back,' she told Robert, still unable to look at him properly.

'He'll be married by now, I expect?'

'No, Paul is the proverbial rolling stone who refuses to gather moss.' In fact her brother had a more off than on and very volatile relationship with a woman friend who was divorced with two small children and who had told him plainly and bluntly that, while she enjoyed going to bed with him, she had no intentions of prejudicing her children's se-

curity by introducing into their lives a man who
was only going to play at being there for them.

'And you...I hear that you're still single as well.'

His comment jarred, reminding her of so many
things she did not wish to remember.

'These days women don't need to marry to lead
fulfilled lives, and at thirty——'

'You're still young enough not to have to worry
too much about the ticking away of your biological
clock. I know,' he agreed, suavely interrupting her.
He had shifted his position somehow so that she
was increasingly aware of him and his effect upon
her senses, and now she turned towards him too
quickly, her eyes widening as she realised just how
close to her he was, as he leaned down towards her,
his eyes only inches from hers as she inadvertently
looked straight at him.

'Strange how things worked out...I'd always
imagined you'd marry young, have children——'

'I don't see why you should be so surprised,' she
interrupted him shakily. 'After all, you were the
one who told me that I'd be a fool to waste my
opportunities, to throw away my chances of success
by tying myself down with a husband and children.'

He *had* said that to her, but they both knew that
what he had meant was that *he* would be a fool if
he threw away *his* chances and tied himself down
by marrying her. But he had deliberately chosen to
make it sound as though he were thinking of her
when in reality his motives had been entirely rooted
in his own needs and wants. If he had thought about
her at all, he would have made sure that she never
got the chance to fall in love with him in the first

place and he would certainly never have allowed her to believe that that love was returned, but then, as she had discovered over the years, men were adept at making women believe they were acting in their best interest and for the most altruistic of reasons when in fact they were doing almost exactly the opposite.

'You've changed, Holly.'

She smiled mirthlessly at him, and said lightly, 'I should think I have, although I prefer to think of it as growth rather than change. I must go, Robert. I've got a board meeting this afternoon and I'm already late.'

She realised as she said it that it sounded more like the defiant boasting of a frightened child than the cool, reasoned comment of a woman too protected and safe from the kind of vulnerability she had once known to be remotely affected by a chance meeting with the man who had once been the cause of her greatest unhappiness.

The look Robert gave her seemed to reinforce her own thoughts.

'Oh, I'm sure they'll wait,' he said softly, and it wasn't a kind comment. 'Odd how different our perceptions are from reality. You're every inch the sleek, sophisticated, successful businesswoman now. I wonder, has she completely obliterated the girl I once knew?'

His comment stunned her. She had no idea what had motivated it or why he should be so deliberately cruel as to mention that girl. He must know how much anguish he had caused her . . . how much pain . . . how much self-revulsion when eventually she had come through the madness of begging and entreating him not to leave her, of pleading tearfully with him to stay...to love her instead of leaving her.

He had changed too...because the Robert she had known would never have made a comment like that. The Robert she had known—the Robert she had *thought* she had known, she reminded herself as she looked away from him, fiercely stabbing the car into gear, and gritting her teeth. But that Robert had never really existed.

As she started to move away, Robert stepped back from the car, telling her drily, 'Next time, remember, set out a bit earlier.'

'Oh, don't worry,' she told him through her gritted teeth. 'Now that I know you've bought this place, wild horses wouldn't drag me within a mile of it.'

Ten minutes later, when she finally pulled out on to the main road, she was still shaking, still cursing herself for her folly in giving in to her need to make that childish verbal defiance. Why on earth hadn't she simply remained cool and uncaring, shrugging aside his comment and just driving off without giving in to the need to react to it?

Well, at least she had made her position plain. As far as she was concerned, his presence in the village wasn't welcome, and she wished he had not chosen to come back. She was glad that it was extremely unlikely that she would have to have any kind of contact with him, although, womanlike, she couldn't help wondering what on earth a single man could possibly want with such a huge barn of a house.

She was of course late for her board meeting, apologising to the other members when she hurried in.

As they discussed the new packaging, she remembered Patsy's hint about Gerald not even being on the board. For some time she had been contemplating inviting him to join them as a non-executive director. He was a well-balanced, cautious man who would help to offset Paul's ebullience, and he was their accountant.

'I hear Robert Graham has just moved into the area,' Lawrence Starling commented to her after the board meeting.

Lawrence was their newly appointed sales manager. Paul had head-hunted him from one of the multi-nationals. Single and two years older than her, he was beginning to develop a semi-proprietorial attitude towards her that Holly was trying to discourage.

'Yes, I believe so,' she agreed dismissively.

'Strange sort of thing for him to do—I mean to move out here...'

'He grew up here,' Holly informed him.

'Oh, I see. Look, Holly, I was wondering: there are one or two aspects of the new packaging I wanted to bring up at the board meeting, but with your being late there really wasn't time. I know Bob Holmes wanted to get off to play golf, and I didn't want to delay him. Could we discuss them over dinner tonight?'

'No, I'm sorry, I already have an engagement,'
Holly told him truthfully. She hadn't missed the
none-too-subtle way Lawrence had let her know
that Bob was playing golf, and, while she was forced
to agree with Paul that Lawrence's aggressive marketing tactics were beginning to pay off, she found
his incessant need to put others down and his un-
curbed ambitious desire both distasteful and
wearying. And besides, in a sense what she had said
was true, even if her engagement was merely with
her garden and her desire to make sure that the new
forget-me-not plants were tucked up in their beds
just as soon as possible.

'Tomorrow, then?' Lawrence pressed her.

Firmly Holly shook her head, telling him, 'I think
you'd better wait and discuss it with Paul when he
gets back. You know that he has overall charge of
marketing.'

The sullen look Lawrence gave her irritated her,
but she didn't let it show. Why was it that men had
this annoying propensity to change from 'I know
best' father figures to sulky little boys whenever the
former bullying manner did not work? Why could
so few men accept a woman as their equal and re-
joice in her success and her skills? Why must they
always feel so threatened and be so antagonistic?
Perhaps it was time that someone discovered a way
of re-programming the entire male species.

If they did, one thing was for sure; it would be
a woman who would make the discovery and implement it...no man would ever admit that his
psyche needed any kind of change.

Reminding herself that she was perhaps being a little unfair and that there were many, many men who were comfortable with and supportive of their female partners' success in life, she headed for her office.

It was six o'clock before she was able to lift her head from her paperwork and think about preparing to go home.

An hour later, as she drove past the entrance to the lane past the Hall, she noticed that two men were working there, putting in the supports for a rough-hewn farm-style gate.

Well, Robert certainly hadn't wasted much time there, she reflected as she put her foot down on the accelerator and sped past.

She was half a mile further down the road when she heard the all too unwanted sound of a police car siren. When she looked in the mirror and saw the driver flashing his lights at her, she cursed under her breath and pulled in to the side of the road.

She *had* been speeding, if only marginally, and she of all people ought to have known better. The number of times she had complained to Paul that he drove too fast— And now *she* was the one to get booked.

The police officer was polite but unrelenting; she wondered what he would have said if she had pleaded in mitigation that it had been the soreness in her heart caused by the memory of an old love-affair that had caused her to put her foot down and break the speed limit. Since he was a man, it was all too probable that he just would not have under-

stood, she told herself as she listened gravely to his
caution. Her first driving offence in over ten years
of blemishless driving. And it was all Robert's fault.

She was still glowering and mentally blaming him
when she eventually drove off, this time keeping a
much stricter eye on her speed.

Rory had gone but the newly turned earth of the
flower-beds showed how hard he had been working.
The forget-me-nots were small dots of soft grey-
green against the darkness of the earth. She lingered
in the garden, studying them, telling them not to
be overawed by their well-established perennial
bedmates, and then paused to console and reassure
those same larger plants, coaxingly promising them
that the new arrivals were no threat to them, and
that the summer extravagance of their pinks, silvers,
whites and blues would be all the more spectacular
after the sharp colour contrast of the bright spring
yellows and blue of the bulbs and forget-me-nots.

It was almost an hour before she had finished
her tour of the garden, and although it was still
light she could smell the crisp early autumn scent
infusing the air.

Yesterday morning she had spotted a heron in-
vestigating the fish pond, which meant that this
weekend she would have to string wires from the
vine eyes in the brick surrounding the pond to stop
him from helping himself to her fish.

The irritation and anxiety produced by her run-
in with Robert was slowly fading as her senses responded to the peace of her garden.

If, ten years ago, someone had told her that she
would become so devoted to such a homely pursuit,

that she would find so much solace and pleasure in it, she would have bitterly denied what they were saying. A small smile touched her mouth. It was time she went in. She was going out this evening.

Their local market town's seventeenth-century assembly rooms had recently been renovated and reopened, providing an elegant setting for a number of events. Tonight's event was a small charity affair; a well-known cellist who supported the charity would be playing for them, and there was to be a light supper afterwards, provided by the local WI.

As a prominent business figure locally, Holly had been approached to support the charity and in addition to buying tickets she had also given a generous donation. The bowls of pot-pourri scenting the rooms had been provided by her company, their perfume a distillation of natural products and one which she personally thought was evocative of the period in which the assembly rooms had been built.

The evening was to be a formal affair—black tie for the men and gowns for the women, preferably with some sort of Regency look about them to complement the setting. When she had originally bought the tickets, Holly had assumed that Paul would be escorting her, but then this trip to South America had intervened.

Instead she was now being partnered by a relative newcomer to the area.

The building of a new private hospital just outside the market town had resulted in an influx of medical personnel. John Lloyd was the new hospital's chief administrator. A Scot in his late thirties, divorced

with two children, he had made no secret of the
fact that he found her very attractive.

However, he was old enough and intelligent
enough to accept that while she enjoyed his
company Holly did not wish their relationship to
progress any further.

For this evening's occasion she had had made an
Empire-style dress in eau-de-Nil silk with silver em-
broidery around the hem. Over it, she was wearing
a dark green velvet cloak lined with the same silk
as the dress. The outfit had been an extravagance,
but, as Paul had pointed out, the event was being
photographed both for the local paper and the
county magazine and she would be photographed
in her role as head of the company so that it was
important that she presented the right appearance.

With the aid of her electric curling-tongs she
managed to produce enough feathery ringlets in her
fine hair to be caught back in a soft ethereal tangle,
vaguely reminiscent of the correct period hairstyle.

When she was dressed and ready, she pulled a
face at herself in her mirror. This kind of event was
not really her style, although the charity in aid of
children in need was one she was more than happy
to support.

Personally she would far rather have made an
anonymous cash donation than participate in this
kind of event, but she quelled these thoughts, telling
herself that she was being very unworldly in
thinking that the money she and others had spent
on outfits for the affair could far more sensibly have
been donated direct to the charity. As Paul had
pointed out to her when she had said as much to

him, there were those who, while they were quite happy to buy expensive tickets for such events, would never have considered donating any such sum without the event to back it up.

John arrived on the dot at half-past seven. Holly didn't invite him in. Years ago she had learned to be wary of naïvely allowing men to mistake her natural warmth and friendliness for sexual encouragement.

After Robert, the heady and dangerous sexual desire he had aroused within her had died completely, leaving her somehow bereft of any ability to respond to men on a sexual basis. As a form of self-preservation it couldn't be beaten, and, in the new restrained mood of sexual constancy and celibacy which seemed to have doused the sexually ferocious fires of earlier decades, she had been able to reflect that perhaps after all Robert had done her a favour in destroying her ability to be sexually responsive to other men.

As she smiled at John and locked the door behind her, he murmured appreciatively, 'Mm...nice perfume.'

Immediately she tensed. She had her back to him, but she could tell from the way she could feel the warmth of his breath against the back of her neck that he was leaning towards her.

'Do you think so? It's our new one,' she told him brightly, firmly stepping to one side and turning round.

'Officially we shan't be launching it for a while yet. It has a floral base, but we've added some subtle extras to bring it into line with current tastes.'

'It's very sexy. And so are you...especially in that dress.'

Hurriedly Holly pulled her cloak more firmly around herself, suddenly uncomfortably conscious of the way the light from the security lights was highlighting the soft pale fullness of her breasts. The dress had a slightly lower neckline than she had expected. She remembered at the time that the dressmaker had pointed out to her that it had been *de rigueur* at the time the Empire line was made so popular for the neckline to reveal the upper curve of the wearer's bosom.

The way John's glance lingered appreciatively on her body made her feel both uncomfortable and irritated. She told herself that she probably ought to feel flattered by his admiration and interest; he was after all a very attractive man but on the one and only occasion when he had taken her in his arms and kissed her she had felt nothing at all, other than a mild sense of curiosity, quickly followed by panic and revulsion when the tenor of his kiss had become too passionate.

And yet with Robert...in Robert's arms... She trembled suddenly, remembering how *he* had made her feel, how her whole body had trembled with eagerness and expectancy. How she had so wantonly and willingly moved closer to him, little moans of anguished expectation filling her throat as her body anticipated the pleasure he would give it. She had given herself to him so eagerly, so naïvely, believing he loved her as she did him. Sexually she might have been inexperienced, but there had been no hesitation in her response to him, no holding back, no restraint, no thought in her head of even attempting to control the emotions he aroused inside her. His merest touch had been enough to send her into a seventh heaven of delirious joy; the lightest brush of his fingertips against her skin, the gentlest touch of his mouth on her lips. And how she had ached for the intimacy of being held close to him without the barrier of their clothes; how she had quivered with longing and need to feel the sensual stroke of his hands on her breasts, her belly... He had cautioned her a little sometimes, groaning against her throat that she made it impossible for him to take his time and to lavish on her all the sensual joy he wanted to give her, because her immediate response to him destroyed his self-control.

She could remember so vividly the first time they had made love; before then there had been kisses and then caresses, so intimate and arousing that she had ached and begged for his complete possession, but he had told her that there was too much risk, that while she was unprotected from an unwanted pregnancy they must be content without that ultimate intimacy.

She could remember even now her first nerve-racking visit to the family-planning clinic, her fear that the doctor would turn down her request, but she had been over eighteen—just, and, although he had eyed her thoughtfully and had spoken to her at great length about her relationship with Robert, eventually she had been given the precious prescription.

She had said nothing to Robert of her decision. He had received her tremulous news in a frowning silence which she had only later recognised should have alerted her to the truth, but then eventually there had come the evening when she had cried and begged him not to hold back, and when he had given in to her whispered pleas and the eager yearning of her body.

They had been lovers for just over six months when he had dropped his bombshell and told her that he would shortly be leaving for America.

She supposed he must have mentioned his decision to accept the post-graduate course at Harvard, but if he had she had deliberately pushed it to the back of her mind, telling herself that their love for one another was bound to be far more important to him than any plans he might previously have made for his career. Their love ... She smiled cynically to herself as she felt the aching shadow of that old pain clutch familiarly at her heart. The love had been all on her side, only she had been too much of a fool to see it. She couldn't blame him for taking physical advantage of that love; after all, she had been the one to instigate that intimacy, to urge and encourage him to make love to her. No, it wasn't his fault that she now found it impossible to experience sexual desire; it was her own, her feelings a direct revulsion against what she felt had been her own lack of self-control, her own inability to face reality, her own stupid self-deception. She was never going to allow herself to fall into that kind of trap again. Never!

'You're very quiet,' John commented as he drove towards their destination. 'Problems at work?'

'No, not really. I was just thinking about the launch of the new perfume,' Holly fibbed.

'But surely that's Paul's responsibility?'

'Yes, it is—at least the launch of the new range is down to him but it was my idea to produce it; we've invested an awful lot of time and money in it...'

'Well, if it makes other women smell as good as you, then I should say from a man's point of view that you've definitely got a winner on your hands.'

Even as she was smiling and accepting his compliment Holly was conscious of an inner dismay, an inner sense of anxiety in case the situation somehow got out of her control. She liked John and she didn't want to lose his friendship, but sexually... She gave a tiny shudder, uncomfortably aware that for some reason seeing Robert this afternoon had heightened and underlined her lack of desire for John to such an extent that she couldn't contemplate him even touching her without experiencing a sharp sense of rejection.

Damn Robert, damn him, she cursed inwardly. Why did he have to come back here? Why?

John parked his car in the market square, empty of stalls and already half full of cars, most of whose occupants were no doubt headed for the same destination.

The assembly rooms were illuminated by discreet floodlights which showed off the newly cleaned stone and the elegance of the Georgian windows and the fanlight above the door.

Holly and John were warmly welcomed by their local MP and her husband. She was on the charity committee and Holly knew her quite well—a woman closer to her mother's age than her own, who was very well thought of locally and who worked hard for the community.

'Holly, I love your dress!' she exclaimed admiringly, adding, 'I'd like to have a word with you later, if I may. We're hoping to organise a Christmas fair to raise some more money, and we shall be looking to local businesses for whatever help they can give.'

Smilingly Holly assured her that they would be pleased to help before walking through into the anteroom to leave her cloak.

The recital was to last two hours with a short break halfway through. Holly and John's seats were close to the front. As they were being directed towards them, a familiar male figure standing talking with another group caught her eye.

She froze immediately, causing John to bump into her and to reach instinctively for her arm as he did so.

Inside Holly could feel herself beginning to tremble. She felt sick and angry at the same time, idiotically close to tears of anger and resentment as she focused on the tall dinner-suit-clad figure of Robert.

He was standing with his back to her, a small dark-haired woman in an expensive designer dress clinging to his side. Holly recognised her immediately as the widow of a local entrepreneur. Although she was in her early forties, she was still a very sensually attractive woman. Too much so, Holly had heard. Apparently she wasn't very well liked by her own sex.

'It's that "helpless little me" act of hers that gets me,' one of Holly's friends had admitted through gritted teeth at a party where Angela Standard had appropriated her husband. 'Especially when I know she's about as helpless as a praying mantis. Everyone knows that she only married Harry Standard for his money. I mean he was close to fifty when they married and she was barely twenty-five . . .'

Then Holly had taken her friend's comments with a pinch of salt, but now she was suddenly so searingly and shockingly jealous that she could easily have crossed the room and torn that pale, clinging hand from Robert's dark-suited arm.

The intensity of her own emotions made her shake inside with sick awareness of how inappropriate and dangerous her feelings were.

She turned away blindly, cannoning straight into John.

'Hey . . . are you OK?'

There was concern and warmth in his voice as he held her. Her eyes blurred with anguished tears, her throat filling with them so that she couldn't speak, shaking her head as she tried to insist that there was nothing wrong. Blindly she pulled away from him, ignoring the curious and speculative look the girl showing them to their seats was giving her.

She felt hot and cold at the same time, sick with an anger that was directed against herself for her idiotic response to the sight of Robert with someone else.

As she sat down in her seat, she tried to tell herself that it was the unexpected shock of seeing him that was responsible for what she was feeling; that if she had anticipated that he might be here and prepared herself for it accordingly she would never have reacted in the way she had; but the arguments failed to convince her, and throughout the first half of the recital she was barely aware of the glorious sounds filling the room, so deeply engrossed was she in her own painful thoughts.

When at the interval John suggested going to the bar for a drink, she shook her head. The last thing she wanted to do was suffer seeing Robert again. She had no idea how on earth she was going to get through the supper following the recital, and wondered if she could possibly plead the excuse of not feeling well in order to escape early.

The thought of having to come face to face with Robert again made her feel sick with tension. Every time she closed her eyes, trying to get control of herself, she was tormented by vivid flashing images of Robert with Angela clinging possessively to his arm.

'If you want a drink, don't let me stop you from having one,' she told John huskily.

'No, it's OK. Look, are you sure you're feeling all right? If you'd like to leave...'

Holly bit down hard on her bottom lip, her guilt increasing with every second. She was behaving like a child...a fool. So Robert was here escorting another woman. She had known for over ten years that he had never loved her the way she had him—had known that and had, or so she thought, come to accept it, so why was she feeling like this now?

During the decade of his absence she had never allowed herself to think about him, to dwell on what he might or might not be doing, and she had thought that the past and her love for him were safely behind her.

People were beginning to return to their seats. The interval was over and with it her opportunity to slip discreetly away.

Throughout the entire second half of the recital panic clawed damagingly at her stomach. She sat tensely on the edge of her seat, sickly wondering how many of the other guests here tonight would remember the love she had once had for Robert. After all, she had never made any attempt to hide it, and many of them were her contemporaries, people with whom she had grown up, people who had known both her and Robert well during their shared youth.

Her close friends had come to accept the fact that she appeared uninterested in men and marriage, putting it down to the fact that the success of her business occupied her time and emotions so fully that there was simply no room in her life for anything or anyone else.

Some of them, she knew, envied her. They told her so openly, contrasting their lives as wives and mothers with what they perceived to be the freedom and excitement of hers, not appearing to realise the discipline her work demanded, the burdens it placed upon her, the responsibilities she had to carry.

But what about those others who would be here tonight, people who knew her less well and were less inclined to see her through the rose-tinted glasses of friendship? Might not they remember the old Holly, the immature, shy girl who so openly and so disastrously adored her lover, who had been too shocked, too distraught when he left her to make any attempt to conceal what she was feeling?

Her closest friends had tried to console her then, telling her that she would soon forget him, coaxing her to try to put the past behind her, and once her pride had fought its way through the anguish that had almost destroyed her she had allowed them to think that they had been right.

She had taught herself not to flinch when people mentioned Robert's name; and even Paul, who was perhaps closer to her than anyone else, had no idea how much the destruction of her dreams still had the power to make her ache inside, even though these days she could acknowledge how foolish and impossible those dreams had been, how flimsy the foundations which had supported them.

But now the one thing she had never allowed herself to contemplate occurring had occurred . . . Robert was back.

But why? When he had left, when he told her about his intention of going to Harvard and from there to climbing the corporate ladder and establishing his own business, he had made it plain to her that he saw his future in the ruling cities of the world—that he saw himself as a man who lived internationally, who called no one place his home, who had neither the need nor the desire for roots.

'But I love you,' Holly had wept, and he had looked at her then, a long, disquieting look that had ripped the scales of self-deceit from her eyes and made her confront the truth.

'You said you loved me,' had been her whispered response to the silent look he gave. 'You said you loved me...'

'Yes, I know,' he had acknowledged quietly. 'But you must understand... I have other needs, other plans.' Such damning, cruel words.

She had cried then, bitter tears of self-betrayal and loss, begging him to retract them, but he had refused.

'You're eighteen, Holly, with your whole life in front of you. You're an intelligent girl. You can't honestly want to tie yourself down now to married life... to children... to the kind of financial and intellectual poverty we'd both suffer if we married now.'

He had hurt her so much and some part of her had believed that she deserved that hurt for being stupid enough to allow herself to believe that when he said he loved her he meant it. She had been merely a brief sexual diversion, that was all—an idiotic, adoring, virginal child with whom he could amuse himself for the brief length of one short summer while he waited for his real life to begin.

She shuddered inwardly, her body writhing in tormented self-disgust as she remembered the way she had behaved... not just when she had learned that he was leaving her, but long, long before that, when she had given herself to him with abandonment and joy, when she had trembled beneath his touch, crying shocked tears of tormented pleasure at the first intimate possession of his body, when she had cried out beneath its masculine heat and thrust, imploring him, begging him to touch her, hold her, fill her with the hard pulse of his male flesh.

There had been no holding back, no self-protective awareness that she was giving him too much, that she might later regret being so open about her feelings for him, her emotional and physical need of him.

That physical abandonment to her desire for him shamed her now as much as her emotional abandonment had done. Even the thought of it was enough to make her tense her muscles, to make her flesh cry out in silent anguished protest at its own weakness. She had sworn then that never, ever again would she allow herself to repeat that kind of self-betrayal.

'Holly, are you all right?'

She realised abruptly that the recital had come to an end, that people were moving in their seats, the room filling with the muted sound of their conversations. Chairs scraped back on the wooden floor, the noise painful to her ears. She felt suddenly as though her senses had been scraped raw, as though she was suffering through them in the same way that one suffered through a raw patch of tender skin.

She badly wanted to shake her head and to tell John that she felt too ill to stay for the supper reception, but her pride wouldn't let her. How would it look if she left now? How many people would put two and two together and make four...would guess that it was because of Robert's presence here that she had fled?

'I'm fine,' she lied. 'Just a bit of a headache, that's all.'

She stood up shakily, an outwardly composed blonde woman who was completely unaware of the attention she was attracting or the reason for it.

Her companion was, though, and he wished for the umpteenth time that he could find a way of breaking down her barriers, of making her respond to him as a man and not just as a friend. She always wore an outer cloak of cool sophistication and calm that was almost immediately belied by the sombreness of her expression, the sadness that always seemed to lurk in her eyes. In so many ways she fascinated and drew him, and not just because of the way she looked. She was always so self-contained, so immaculate, so perfectly poised and turned out that his need to see her with her mouth swollen after love, her hair tangled by his fingers, her eyes languorous and heavy, her breathing quickened, sharp and desirous, was sometimes so great that he ached to reach out and take hold of her. But he knew how unwelcome his sexual attentions would be, how little she wanted him in that kind of way.

There were women who lacked a definite sex-drive and men as well, but for all her coolness, her remoteness he didn't think that Holly was one of them; she reminded him somehow of a child who was burned and who was now afraid of fire.

A group of people were approaching them. John touched Holly's arm to draw her attention to them.

Holly turned her head and immediately tensed. Their local MP was coming towards them, smiling warmly at them, and behind her, along with two or three other people, was Robert . . . and of course Angela.

'Holly. There you are. You must remember Robert? Yes, of course you do. He and Paul were good friends, weren't they? You'll have heard of course that he's bought the Hall?

'I'm trying to persuade him to let us use the minstrel's gallery there for a performance by the local madrigal society. It would be such a wonderful setting.'

'Not right now, it wouldn't,' Holly heard Robert saying drily. 'The place is full of woodworm and just about to be sprayed against its spread.'

Everyone was laughing. Angela clung possessively to Robert's arm. Didn't she realise how ridiculous she looked—a woman of her age? Even if she was a very, very attractive and feminine forty-odd. Stop it, Holly warned herself. Stop it at once.

She forced her lips to frame a smile, the kind of smile she had so painstakingly learned to put on the public face those occasions when she had to appear as one of the new successful women of the nineties. It was a calm, cool smile, the kind of smile that said yes, she knew she was successful, and that yes, she knew she was attractive, and that she had the self-confidence in herself to carry off both these assets without the need to flaunt them like banners of war in the face of those who were less fortunate.

She could see Angela glancing dismissively at her, her own smile a definite cat-that-got-the-cream smile, a sensual, satisfied smile that said quite positively, 'Yes, I'm all woman and he's all man—and mine.'

Holly deliberately avoided looking directly at Robert, saying as calmly as she could, 'Hello, Robert.'

'Holly...'

No mention of their meeting earlier in the day, no comments about her success... her metamorphosis from shy teenager into successful woman of the world; but then what had she expected—that he would take one look at her and immediately announce that he had always regretted leaving her, that not a single day had passed without him wanting her?

As she touched John lightly on the arm, and excused them both to their hostess, fibbing that she was starving and longing to get to the buffet, she derided herself inwardly for her stupidity.

It was over, finished, and had been for over a decade. There was no point, no purpose in her continuing to torment herself like this... none whatsoever. So why did she?

CHAPTER THREE

WHY indeed?

Holly was, she discovered ten minutes later when she and John walked into the room set aside for supper, still fighting her reaction to that brief meeting. As she spotted Patsy and Gerald on the other side of the room, Patsy turned her head and saw them, hurrying over to speak to her.

Why on earth had she ever thought the neckline of her own dress might be considered too low? Holly wondered with a brief resurgence of her normal sense of humour as she glanced briefly at the outrageously *décolleté* dress that Patsy was wearing. The chiffon skirt of the dress was so fine that it was almost possible to see right through it.

'That's how they wore them in those days,' Patsy told her defensively after she had admired Holly's outfit and then drawn her attention to her own. 'They used to damp down their skirts so that they would cling to their bodies.'

'I know,' Holly agreed drily. 'I read Georgette Heyer as well, you know.'

Patsy giggled. 'Mm...poor Gerald, I don't think he'd have looked too good in a pair of tight pantaloons, do you? Come to think of it, not many of the men here would.' The two women had drawn slightly apart from the men. Holly had her back to them, and so she was caught off guard, when Patsy suddenly whispered in her ear, 'Mind you, Robert would. He's the epitome of a Regency hero, don't you think? All tough maleness . . . dark-haired and brooding, don't you agree?'

She really couldn't help it; even before her conscious mind knew what she was doing she had turned her head and had focused on the small group attracting Patsy's attention.

Robert had his back to her and was apparently deeply engrossed in conversation with Gerald, but, as though he knew that she was watching him, he turned round and looked at her.

Her heart seemed to turn a somersault and then stop beating altogether. She was vaguely aware of the hum of conversation around her, a noise like distant bees, numbing her thought processes so that her whole world was narrowed down to this one man, this one heartbeat in time.

An odd feeling of being drawn physically into danger, of being powerless to stop herself from walking towards him overwhelmed her, further weakening her. She focused on his eyes, the pupils of her own dilating, her breath quickening, her whole body tensing.

And then abruptly the spell was broken as Patsy stepped in between them, pouting flirtatiously up at Robert as she exclaimed, 'Robert! How lovely to see you again. Holly and I were just saying that of all the men here you're the only one who could possibly do justice to our fantasies of a sexy Regency rake.'

She was smiling provocatively at him, her hand on his sleeve, smoothing away an invisible piece of

thread, either deliberately ignoring or oblivious to
the killing looks she was receiving from Angela.
Knowing Patsy, Holly suspected that it was the
former. She glanced at Gerald. He was watching
his wife with an expression that was a cross between resignation and irritation. Poor man, but if
he hadn't learned by now that Patsy would never
change, that flirtation was as necessary to her as
breathing, then he never would.

'Yes, Holly was just saying how much she would
love to see you wearing a pair of those tight-knitted
pantaloon things they used to wear in those days,'
she heard Patsy saying outrageously as she batted
her eyelashes up into Robert's impassive face.

At any other time, with any other man, Holly
doubted if she would have felt anything other than
a very mild irritation at her friend's comment, but
here and now and with this man the feelings that
convulsed drove the hot colour burningly up under
her pale skin and forced her to bite down hard on
the fierce denial she ached to utter, knowing that
such a passionate disclaimer would do more harm
than good, that indifference and amusement were
her best form of defence.

The others were all looking at her now, as well
they might be, Holly recognised. Never had she
wished more strongly for her brother's presence.
He was more than a match for Patsy, who was not
the sort to be deliberately malicious, but who was
nevertheless heedless sometimes of other people's
feelings.

At her side, John gave her a wry look and murmured, 'I'd no idea you entertained fantasies of Regency rakes...'

'I don't,' Holly denied shortly. 'You know Patsy...'

At any other time, she would have been amused by the way that Angela had now manoeuvred herself to Robert's other side, so that he had a woman clinging to either arm. He was carrying off the situation very well, she had to admit, neither appearing to be embarrassed nor flattered by the attention he was receiving.

Gerald muttered something about his purchase of the Hall and Robert replied that there was a good deal of work to be done inside the house.

'And outside it as well. The gardens need completely redesigning and replanting.'

'Well, if you want some expert advice there, you can't do any better than to enlist Holly's help,' Gerald told him enthusiastically. 'The garden at the farm has to be seen to be believed. She's truly worked miracles with it.'

'Yes, it's a real credit not just to her eye for colour and line but to her hard work as well,' John chimed in while Holly writhed inwardly in embarrassment, aching to be able to escape.

'Oh, a cottage garden's one thing,' Angela announced disdainfully, 'but the Hall calls for something quite different and someone who's been properly trained and has the appropriate qualifications. An amateur, no matter how enthusiastic, is hardly the right sort of person to deal with such an important project.'

Which put *her* well and truly in her place, Holly reflected to herself.

Suddenly, no matter what it might cost her in the terms of the kind of speculation people might make, she knew she couldn't stay any longer.

Turning to John, she said brittly, 'Would you mind if we left, John?'

'Of course not. Is it the headache?' he asked her solicitously. 'You wait here. I'll go and get your cloak.'

Before she could protest that she would accompany him, he had gone, leaving her with no option but to wait where she was.

'Any firm news yet about when Paul will be back?' Gerald asked her while she waited for John to return.

She shook her head. 'No, although he will definitely be back in time for the new perfume launch.'

As he turned from her to Robert, she heard Gerald saying proudly, 'I expect you'll have heard how well Holly's business is doing.'

'Yes, indeed.'

The enigmatic look that accompanied the words made her tense.

At his side Angela interjected nastily, 'Well, of course, it's all just a fad, isn't it—this natural green thing? And, while Holly and Paul are to be congratulated for jumping on the bandwagon so quickly, no one really believes that it's a fashion that's going to last...'

There was a small sharp silence, and although she was inwardly seething Holly contented herself with giving the older woman a coolly thoughtful

look, not wanting to precipitate any unpleasantness by crisply telling her just why her views
were not only biased but also uninformed and
blinkered.

She was just about to turn away and excuse
herself to go in search of John, when to her aston-
ishment Robert spoke, saying firmly, 'I think you're
wrong, Angela, and, from what I've heard, far
from jumping on any bandwagon, Holly's been one
of the market leaders in her field, and is to be congratulated on having the tenacity and the deter-
mination to follow through on her own principles
instead of allowing herself to be swayed by other
market forces. There aren't many people these days
who are prepared to put their personal beliefs before
profits.'

'There are more of us than you think,' Holly
corrected him, unable to remain silent, so strongly
did she feel on this particular subject. 'And a lot
of us are women.'

Robert's eyebrows rose.

'A rather sexist remark.'

'A statement based on fact,' Holly corrected him.
'Women are more in touch with their feelings than
men—that *is* a fact; they are more aware of the
dangers of further damage to our environment. It
is, after all, women who bear and nurture each new
generation, and who therefore have the strongest
desire to protect it and its environment.'

'I could take issue with you on that,' Robert told
her. 'Men are equally protective of their young,
albeit perhaps in a different way. After all, we are

all of us on this planet together, male and female, rich and poor.'

Without realising how it had happened, Holly suddenly discovered that the two of them had become separated from the others and were standing alone, and surely Robert was standing far closer to her than he had been before. She had forgotten how tall he was, how masculine and powerful, and how fragile and female he had always made her feel.

A tiny shudder of self-loathing ripped through her as she fought down her instinctive impulse to move closer to him. Sickened by her self-betrayal, she deliberately forced herself to step back from him, tensing her spine in rejection of her own weakness.

As she turned her head, she saw John coming towards her, carrying her cloak.

Relief flooded through her. She was already starting to walk towards him when Robert stunned her by saying quietly, 'Oh, and by the way, I should appreciate your advice on the gardens if you could spare the time to look over them.'

'How are you feeling now?' John was asking her anxiously, helping her on with her cloak as she battled in silence with her shock at Robert's request for her help.

As John started to say goodbye to the others, Robert added, 'I'll be in touch...about the garden.' And then John was ushering her away, solicitously putting his arm around her.

Later she reflected that she must have made conversation with John on the way home or at least responded normally enough to his comments because when he finally left her at her front door he seemed to be completely unaware of her turmoil and shock.

Once inside, once alone, once she was free of the necessity to keep up a front, she sank down in front of her sitting-room fire, her head in her hands, her whole body shaking with the release from tension.

Her entire body ached from the stress she had put on her muscles. She felt physically tired... physically battered almost, feverish and weak, like someone suffering from a physical disease.

She had recently had a gas fire installed in her sitting-room—less authentic than an open coal or wood-burning hearth, but easier to keep clean, and instantly warm and comforting, she reflected gratefully as she turned it on.

She was so cold inside, as though her stomach were filled with ice. She started to shiver, hugging her arms around her body, her brain acknowledging that what she was suffering was the fall out of the intense shock of seeing Robert, while her emotions tried frantically to reject that knowledge.

She didn't *want* to be affected like this by him. She didn't *want* to be dragged back into the past, to suffer again what she had suffered then. She wanted to forget he had ever existed... to forget that he had ever made her feel...

She swallowed hard, her throat sore and swollen with tension as she fought against remembering just *how* he had made her feel, just how he had aroused within her such an intensity of emotional and

physical responsiveness that even now, over ten
years later, the memory of it was as fresh and sharp
as though it had only been yesterday.

Even to think of him now was enough to make
her muscles tense, her breasts ache, her body
tremble ... her mouth soften. If she closed her eyes
now, it would be so easy to remember, to pretend...
The totally unexpected sound of someone ringing
her doorbell jerked her back to reality.

As she scrambled to her feet, wincing as she felt
the pins and needles in her numb flesh, she realised
how long she had been sitting motionless in front
of the fire, lost in her memories of the past.

The hall was in darkness. She switched on the
lights that were on the wall, the ceilings being too
low to support central lights. The exposed beams
in the walls had a soft sheen in the light, the peachy
tinged plasterwork giving off a mellow warmth.

Paul had told her she was mad when she had
informed him that she planned to carpet her hall
in the same soft peach as the walls, but she had
ignored his comments and the effect was both warm
and welcoming.

A couple of thick rugs strategically placed took
the brunt of the wear plus any grime accidentally
walked in by visitors and the good-quality underlay
recommended by the carpet suppliers softened the
uncomfortable hardness of the concrete damp-
proof course that lay directly beneath it.

As she opened the heavy oak door, she remembered guiltily how often Paul had told her to get a
safety-chain, but it was already too late. The door

was open and the man standing outside with his back to the door was turning towards her.

She had recognised him long before she saw his face. After all, hadn't she once known his body so intimately that there was no angle at which she might view it and not instantly recognise it?

'Robert...'

Her voice shook as she said his name.

'I had to come this way home after dropping Angela off, and I thought I'd call in and see how you were feeling. I take it your friend isn't still here?'

Her friend? It took her a few seconds to realise that he meant John and then another few to realise that out of self-protection if nothing else she ought to have seized on the chance Robert was offering her and told him that he was, but by then it was too late—she was already shaking her head, already stepping back into the hallway so that he could enter the house.

'I...I was just about to go to bed,' she told him untruthfully once he was inside, and then immediately flushed an uncomfortable bright red as he looked directly at her.

For a pulsebeat of time she was vividly reminded of a time when to be alone with him like this would have instantly meant that she was in his arms, pressing her body eagerly against his, whispering to him how much she loved him, how much she wanted him.

'I shan't keep you. As I said, I was driving past, and I saw that the light was on downstairs. I remembered the migraines you used to get, and how you used to say that having your scalp massaged was always a far more effective cure than pain-killers.'

Holly stared at him. Was she actually hearing what she thought she had heard? It was true that she had always claimed that massage worked better than pain-killers, but only because of the pleasure it gave her to have him touch her, and the thought that he could actually be suggesting that he had called round here to offer her that kind of panacea now, after the way they had parted . . . when they hadn't seen one another in over a decade, seemed so implausible as to make her think she must be imagining having heard it.

When she finally mustered the self-control to be able to look at him, he was watching her questioningly as though waiting for some kind of response. A wave of giddy recklessness swept over her, a sharp, splintering desire to encourage the delusion which seemed to have possessed her, a dangerous impulse to allow herself to believe what she had heard, to whisper to him that there was nothing she wanted more than to feel his hands on her skin; a warm, wanton feminine urge to allow herself to drift along on whatever roller-coaster of fate had brought him to her door tonight, but then thankfully sanity intervened.

'It isn't a migraine,' she told him, recognising both the panic in her own voice and the longing, and hoping that he wouldn't recognise them as well.

For a woman of thirty she was behaving in a ridiculously immature fashion. Heavens, how many times in the last decade had she had to deal with unwanted male attentions and had dealt with them with far more aplomb and sophistication than she was showing now? But then of course she had known what she was confronting. Here... She closed her eyes. She must be going mad...must be imagining what Robert had said...must be a victim of her own idiocy.

He could not have said, could not have implied...

'And as I said, I was just on my way to bed,' she reiterated shakily, trying now to do what she should have done before, which was to get him out of the house before she betrayed herself completely.

The way he was watching her made her tremble.

'It's all right, Holly, I can take a hint.'

He was turning towards the door but then abruptly he turned back so that she almost cannoned into him.

'You're sure you're feeling all right?'

'Yes. Yes, I'm feeling fine.' She was practically gabbling in her desperate need to get him out of her home.

'Why are you trembling so much, then?'

The soft question stilled her agitated movements.

'I'm...I'm not,' she lied protestingly.

'Yes—yes, you are. I can feel it..'

The shock of suddenly finding herself in his arms, of suddenly being held lightly against his body, the wholly unexpected intimacy of what was happening defeated her ability to reason. She could only stand there while he held her, her eyes blank with shock and disbelief as his hands ran gently down her arms and then up over her back, and his voice murmured softly against her ear.

'I shouldn't be here, should I, Holly? You want
to go to bed, and you want me to leave.'

He was still holding her. His head turned, his
mouth touching hers in the gentle, altruistic kiss of
a friend, a brother. She was transfixed with disbelief, with the pain of thinking that she must be
imagining what was happening.

Beneath the light caress of his lips hers trembled.
She could feel the deep burning sensation of pain
growing inside her.

Once before he had kissed her like this, on her
seventeenth birthday... Her first kiss. The kiss of
an older male for a friend's younger sister. Then
she had clung to him in mindless ecstasy, silently
pleading for more... now...

She started to move away and instantly he
stopped her, one hand lifting to her head, sliding
into her hair, holding her a prisoner, not by force,
but by the sensual stroke of his hand, the slow, sure
caress of his mouth.

It was as though the whole world was caving in
around her, burying her in some subterranean place
from which there was no escape from the burden
of agonising pleasure he was enforcing on her. How
well her senses remembered that pleasure, how
easily they responded to it, recognising it, yearning
for it...

She could feel her self-control starting to slide
away from her, knew that in another handful of
seconds she would be clinging to him, silently
begging for him.

A shudder racked through her as she pulled
herself away from him.

'You had no right to do that,' she stormed furiously at him, too distressed to hide what she was feeling.

'No right at all,' she heard him agreeing quietly. 'No right, but every need. I've often wondered what manner of woman you'd turn into, Holly.' His mouth twisted in a smile she found it hard to understand.

'I've never realised until now what a poor thing my imagination is. John—is he your lover?'

She reacted instinctively, shaking her head in immediate and angry denial and then recognising too late the danger she was courting as she added huskily, 'My private life has nothing to do with you.'

'No? We were once lovers,' he reminded her.

The shock of hearing him put it into words was like a knife in her flesh, the pain instant and deathly.

'That...that was over ten years ago,' she managed to stammer.

'Eleven years and ten months,' he told her as he opened the door. He was halfway through it when he paused and said coolly, 'You won't forget your promise to come and look over the gardens, will you?'

Her *promise*? She had not given any *promises*. She opened her mouth to say as much, but it was too late, he had gone, closing the door behind him.

For a long time she simply stayed where she was, trying to make sense of what had happened.

For him to call round at all was so unexpected, so...so...at odds with the behaviour she had ex-

pected from him. But then, to have touched her,
to have kissed her, to have implied that he... That
he what? That he found her desirable as a woman?
Was she going mad? How *could* he possibly find
her desirable *now* when he had told her quite ca-
tegorically and very cruelly that he neither wanted
nor loved her.

What was he trying to do? It must be some kind
of sick joke. Holly couldn't think of any other explanation for his behaviour. Perhaps he had become
the kind of man whose vanity would not allow him
to permit any woman who had once loved him to
cease doing so? There were such men, or so she had
heard. But vanity had never been one of his weak-
nesses...especially not that kind of vanity. But what
other explanation could there be? Men like him
simply did not behave the way he had behaved, they
did not walk into a woman's house and hold her
in their arms, touching and kissing her, intimating
that they wanted her—at least not unless they were
very, very sure that their advances would be
welcomed.

Robert was a sophisticated, mature man, and no
doubt used to playing sophisticated sexual games,
but what on earth had motivated him to start
playing them with her? He must surely know that
he was the last person she would ever want back in
her life...the last man she would ever allow herself
to become involved with. If he wanted casual sex,
she suspected that Angela Standard would have
been only too pleased to oblige him, and if he
thought for one moment that because she had *once*
been vulnerable and stupid enough to love him that

he could simply walk back into her life and she was going to fall into his arms all over again, then he could damn well think again.

All right, so he might have caught her off guard tonight, but from now on she was going to make it plain to him that she wasn't interested in any kind of game-playing, and that the vulnerable girl she had once been had gone forever, destroyed by his cruelty.

But when she finally lay in bed she could still feel the warmth of his mouth on hers, still feel the betraying tingle of sensation that had torn through her, still feel the small betraying ache deep within her body as it cried out its need for him.

Panic gripped her. This couldn't be happening. She must not let it happen. She wasn't going to fall in love with him all over again. She must not fall in love with him all over again. Hadn't she learned anything from the past... anything at all? Must she remind herself again of every pain he had inflicted on her... the agony she had suffered when he'd left her?

CHAPTER FOUR

IT WAS the low insistent burr of the bedside telephone that eventually woke Holly, bringing her to
the shocking realisation that she had somehow slept
right through her alarm and that it was now gone
nine o'clock.

Oversleeping was something she did not do normally, but then suddenly nothing about her life was
normal any more, and last night, after shutting the
door behind Robert, she had somehow omitted to
close the door of her mind against him as well so
that her sleep had been punctuated by intensely
vivid dreams of him, which had carried her back
to the past, to a time when they had been lovers,
when she had believed he loved her. Perhaps after
all it was not so surprising then that, when she had
eventually fallen into a dreamless sleep, that sleep
had been unusually deep.

She reached for the telephone receiver, groggily
saying her name.

'Are you all right?' she heard John asking her
anxiously. 'I've just rung your office and they said
you weren't in. After last night...'

Immediately she tensed. How did John know that
Robert had come round to see her? How did...?

'You looked so ill when we left the assembly
rooms.'

70

Abruptly she realised that John had no idea that Robert had called round to see her and that he was in actual fact referring to her supposed illness during supper. Guilt and despair tensed her body as she reassured him shakily, 'I'm fine, John. I overslept, that's all.'

'I had thought we might have lunch together,' he told her.

'No, I'm sorry, I can't. I've got a planning meeting I can't get out of.'

It was the truth and yet as she replaced the receiver she was conscious of a guilty feeling of relief that she had had the excuse. What was the matter with her? John was an intelligent and pleasant man, a man whose company and conversation she had always enjoyed, and yet here she was, relieved to have an excuse to turn down his invitation. *Why*?

Her reactions were so unfamiliar to her, so emotionally charged and unstable, and, like her mood-swings, more like those of a teenager than a mature woman.

She paused halfway out of bed, shivering a little. Oh, no, she wasn't going back down that road again. She was over Robert. It was finished ... finished. She had learned her lesson the hard way; all right, so she might still be vulnerable, susceptible to the past ... but that was all it was. She was a different person now. A wiser, saner person, a woman and not a child, and as a woman she recognised the danger of allowing herself to be drawn into a situation which might ignite her emotional vulnerability to him.

She would give him a wide berth, make sure that she had as little contact with him as possible. After all, a person predisposed to some inherited and fatal disease did not go courting the very thing that would activate that disease, did they? It was better to be cautious now, to evade any kind of confrontation, any kind of challenge.

But why should Robert want to challenge her? Why should he want to have anything to do with her? He had made it plain enough how he felt about her when he left, hadn't he?

But last night he had touched her . . . kissed her . . . implied——

Implied what? she demanded of herself aggressively as she forced her body into action and headed for her bathroom. What exactly was it that he had implied? That he found her sexually desirable?

How could he? He must have been playing some kind of cruel game with her, testing her. The best thing she could do was to ignore him completely, to pretend that he simply did not exist. He would soon tire of tormenting her then and turn his attentions to someone else.

And after all he wouldn't have to look far to find someone far more responsive to him— Angela, for instance . . .

Fortunately her planning meeting wasn't scheduled to begin until eleven o'clock but once she was showered she took the opportunity of ringing her PA to let her know she had been delayed.

'What happened?' Alice asked her anxiously. 'John rang and he said that you hadn't been at all well last night.'

'A combination of too rich a diet of both music and food,' Holly fibbed, 'but I'm feeling fine now. I'll be in in time for the planning meeting.'

She walked into her bedroom to replace the receiver, catching a glimpse of herself in the full-length mirror as she did so. With her wet and tousled hair and her face free of make-up, the image reflected back at her made her wrinkle her nose and pull a face at herself.

It had been a good summer and her skin was slightly tanned from working in the garden, although, being so fair-skinned, she was careful always to keep her face protected from its harmful rays.

On a not altogether understood impulse, she abruptly let go of her towel, studying her naked reflection in the mirror.

Her body was taut and firm, partially as a result of her gardening and partially as a result of the exercise class she forced herself to attend once a week—as much for its benefits as a means of reducing tension as for keeping her body well toned.

She wasn't an exercise junkie, but believed that every individual owed it to themselves to take the best possible care they could of their health, and consequently her skin had the sheen and elasticity of someone who paid sensible attention to her diet, her hair and eyes glowing with good health. She was slim-hipped and narrow-waisted, with slender legs, and if she privately considered that her breasts were fuller than she would have liked she had grown adept at choosing clothes that minimised rather than maximised that fullness.

As a woman she looked upon her body much as a piece of equipment which in order to function properly needed to be properly maintained.

To be healthy and energetic were more important to her than how her body looked, and yet now almost inadvertently she found herself wondering how a man would view her. As a teenager, her flesh had been softer, rounder; Robert, she remembered, had loved to touch her, to stroke her skin with his fingertips, to kiss her—and not just on her lips. He had kissed her throat, her breasts, her belly, the narrow indentation of her waist, the vulnerable smooth flesh of her inner thighs, caressing her as though he loved the taste and the feel of her.

She had kissed him in turn, but more shyly, more hesitantly, always a little in awe of his body... of him.

She remembered how when he had wanted to caress her intimately with his mouth she had refused to let him, shocked by what he was suggesting, withdrawing from him in tense agitation. He had let her go, not pushing or coercing her; and then instead he had caressed her breasts, gently sucking on her nipples until she twisted against him, crying out in a swiftly spiralling coil of need.

Close at hand she could hear someone breathing erratically. She had closed her eyes, but now she opened them quickly, realising immediately that it was her own breathing she could hear. In the mirror she saw the way her breasts were rising and falling in quickened agitation, her nipples swollen and erect. A tiny shudder ran through her as she fought against her awareness of her body's arousal, quickly turning away from the mirror image of her naked body, not wanting to acknowledge the flush of heat that stained her skin, the ache of need that pulsed through her.

Almost as though to compensate for what she was feeling, for her vulnerability as a woman, she dressed in a suit she had bought on impulse and which almost immediately she had recognised to be a mistake.

It was too severely cut for her slender frame, looking almost caricaturishly masculine on her, its dull beige colour unflattering to her very English skin.

Once downstairs, knowing she was running late, she made herself a healthy drink in the blender, mentally going through the points on the agenda for the planning meeting.

The sales department were pressing for more new products, but she intended to stand firmly by her decision not to market any product until she herself had complete faith in it—better to keep their product base small than to expand into lines which prejudiced the company's stance on environmental and other issues, she had informed the sales department.

Hopefully once Paul returned from South America they could begin more detailed research on new products, using the information he had gathered there. The sales department were really Paul's responsibility and tended to respond better to him than they did to her, even though right from the start she had insisted that where possible she wanted only sales people who shared her commitment to the environment.

All the sales force drove vehicles that ran on lead-free fuel and all of them were instructed to keep their business mileage as low as possible. To prove her point she had taken them all into the nearest city one busy Friday afternoon and made them stand at a large traffic intersection, breathing in the fumes from the traffic, reminding them as she did so that children and babies who were so much closer to those fumes were so much more at risk from the effects of them.

She arrived at the factory and office complex on the outskirts of town at half-past ten, deftly parking her car in the space allocated for it, before getting out and locking it.

The lease of the property had been expensive, and Paul had suggested that a new modern purpose-built unit on another industrial estate would be more economical. However, Holly had insisted on going ahead with the lease here because this development had involved the refurbishment of an old and neglected mill, running alongside a narrow, dank and uncared-for section of a local canal, and she had approved of the fact that here not only was an attempt being made to upgrade a very neglected eyesore, but also that the renovation of the mill would involve the recycling of material and the minimum usage of new materials; and her foresight had paid off in a variety of unexpected ways, not the least of which, according to their PR department, being the good Press her foresight had gained for them.

A small enclave of craftspeople had also sprung up in smaller units of the mill: an enterprising local couple had opened a health-food bar and restaurant with canal frontage, and now what had once been a contaminated stretch of water filled with the debris of modern-day living in the form of rusting cycles, washing machines and the like was now a calm stretch of living water whose far reeded banks were home to a variety of waterfowl.

An atrium had been created in the centre of the mill, and the boardroom overlooked this atrium, with Holly's adjacent office overlooking the canal itself.

Alice, her PA, looked up with a smile as she walked in, her smile fading betrayingly as she saw what Holly was wearing.

'I know. Not one of my better buys,' Holly agreed with Alice's silent condemnation as she took off her jacket. 'I must admit, I never thought I'd ever become a victim of media hype. I seem to remember I bought this suit after reading a spate of articles on power-dressing. Anything important in the post?'

'Nothing urgent,' Alice told her. 'There's a rather interesting letter from a grower, asking if you'd be interested in organically grown lavender, and another from someone wanting to know if you'd be interested in buying her great-grandmother's recipe for hand-cream.

'We've also started to get back the results on the tests for the avocado face cream.'

'And?'

'And so far so good. Apparently everyone who tried it liked it and so far no one has reported any adverse reactions, although one woman has written that her husband liked the taste of it so much, he thought it should be turned into a body lotion.'

They both laughed, and then Alice offered, 'Coffee?'

'Mm . . . yes, please.'

It was a standing joke that, despite several attempts to do so, Holly had never been able to overcome her love of strong coffee. Every now and again she would switch to a decaffeinated variety, only to switch back again when her taste-buds craved the flavour of a more robust brew.

The planning meeting went off without any hitches, although Holly was wryly aware of the surreptitious glances her male colleagues kept giving her suit.

It certainly was making an impact on them, she acknowledged, although she wasn't too clear exactly what the impact was until the meeting ended and as they were all filing out of the boardroom the head of their PR department hesitated, hanging back to ask her uncertainly, 'That suit...you aren't planning to wear it for the new launch, are you, Holly?'

Giving him a bland smile, she fibbed, 'I don't know. I might. Why?'

He coughed and looked embarrassed, shuffling from one foot to the other before saying uneasily, 'Well, it's just that I thought perhaps something a little softer... a different colour.'

Gravely telling him she would bear his comments in mind, Holly closed the boardroom door and then walked through into her own office.

'Something wrong?' Alice asked her, seeing her frown.

'No, not really. I was just wondering if men would ever stop judging women by their appearance and when they would start valuing us as people, as human beings.'

Now it was Alice's turn to frown, and Holly shook her head in resignation.

'Oh, don't pay any attention to me, Alice. I think I must be getting old.'

The phone rang as she was speaking. Alice answered it and then told her, 'Elaine Harrison from London.'

Elaine Harrison was the executive from the PR agency whom the company employed to handle their public image—an innovation of Paul's that Holly had never felt entirely comfortable with, even though she liked Elaine herself very much.

'Put her through,' she told Alice now, smiling warmly as she picked up her own receiver and said, 'Elaine, hello.'

'Hi. Look, I need to see you about the PR coverage for the new perfume. I know it's short notice, but could I come up this afternoon? If you're free we could discuss things over dinner tonight and then I could travel back to London in the morning.'

Holly hesitated, reaching for her diary, even though she knew already that her evening was free. The trouble was that she hated this aspect of her

business so much, hated being in the public
eye ... and felt uncomfortable with the fact that the
public associated the company so strongly with her.

She had complained to Elaine that she sometimes felt she was being turned into the token ordinary woman made good—that she sometimes felt
as though she was little more than a doll to be
paraded in front of the world as a symbol of a successful businesswoman who had still retained her
femininity ... her roots.

Elaine had sympathised, but pointed out that that
was life, in the business world at least; that you
would never get a male head of a company refusing
to capitalise on any asset which would increase the
profitability of that business.

'Maybe not,' Holly had agreed, adding with un-
characteristic bitterness, 'But then you don't get
many male executives being interviewed all dressed
up in designer clothing with their hair and faces
tortured into some photographer's idea of fashion
and then portrayed as objects of wonder simply because they retain their masculinity while being
successful.'

Elaine had laughed and then shaken her head,
telling her drily, 'Make the most of the way you
look, Holly. You can't imagine how many successful women I have to deal with who are virtually
reduced to tears because they don't fit into the accepted stereotype of what makes a woman feminine
and desirable, women who are petrified that their
plain ordinariness will reflect badly on their
business.

'I know we'd all like to be judged on our abilities and not our looks, but unfortunately life isn't like that and some of the worst offenders are other members of our own sex.'

'I am free this evening,' Holly told Elaine now, adding cautioningly, 'But you know how I feel about the media circus.'

'Yes, I know,' Elaine agreed soothingly. 'But this is an important step forward for you...for the company. I know how strongly you believe in your products, Holly. Surely it isn't asking too much for you to tell the world that.'

If only it were as easy as that, Holly reflected wryly ten minutes later when she had replaced the receiver.

Elaine was very clever and persuasive, and it was after all her job to ensure that the new perfume range got the maximum media coverage.

Right from the start Holly had insisted that she did not want her products advertised by impossibly glamorous models whose image was all too likely to make other women feel inadequate and inferior, that she wanted her products to speak for themselves, but she hadn't envisaged then that that would involve her in so much media work.

'Elaine will be arriving later this afternoon,' she told Alice now. 'Could you book her a room at Sarle Manor, please, Alice? Oh, and you'd better book us a table for this evening at Alistair's.'

Midway through the afternoon she received a totally unexpected phone call from her brother. The international line was surprisingly clear, and for some unexplained reason the sound of Paul's cheerful voice brought a lump to Holly's throat and a tiny ache to her heart. She and Paul, opposites in so many ways, were very close in others, and she had missed him this summer.

They discussed the launch of the new perfume for a few seconds, and then he told her, 'I think I've got one or two things here that are going to prove extremely interesting. I want to get them back to the UK, to do some proper research on them; that means going through the whole performance of import and export licences, of course. I've got all that in hand, but you know what it's like. I could be tied up here for another few weeks. Oh, and by the way, I've taken a look at your baby. Want to know how it's doing?'

Holly grimaced at the teasing note in his voice. The male executives had been dubious at first when she had announced that the company was going to buy and protect an acreage of rain forest, but she had been so determined to go ahead that she had told them she would pay for it herself, if they refused to sanction the company's purchase.

In the end they had given way, and even though it had upset her later to discover that someone had leaked their decision to the Press she had told herself that the good public relations benefits of their decision did not detract from the value of what they were doing for the environment, even though she personally would have preferred to keep their purchase out of the public eye. She was sensitively conscious that it could look as though her decision had been taken for purely commercial reasons, for the benefits that would accrue to the company in being seen to do something positive for the environment—and that was something to which she was totally opposed . . . just as she was insistent that whenever the company made a charitable donation it was made anonymously.

'Look, I don't want to say too much over the phone, but I've got some really interesting stuff here, and just as soon as I've got the formalities sorted out I'll be on my way home.'

'I hope you're going to be back in time for the launch,' Holly warned him.

'Don't worry. I'll be there. Any news? Anything interesting happening?'

Holly paused, and then told him reluctantly, 'Not really. Only one thing . . . Robert Graham is back. He's bought the Hall.'

'Has he? Good old Robert. I remember he always did have rather a yen for the old place.'

A sharp, unexpected pain stabbed through Holly. Robert had never told her that. Had never confided that to her . . . had never shared it with her.

Later, as she prepared to leave the office, she told herself that it was just another reinforcement of what she already knew—that she had never meant anything at all to Robert. That she had just been a silly girl, whom he had used sexually, allowing her to believe that he loved her because it suited him to do so, when in reality . . .

Don't, she warned herself as she drove home. Don't think about him. He doesn't matter. He's out of your life and that's where he's going to stay.

And yet, as she unlocked her front door, her tongue-tip touched her lips as though seeking the sensation of his moving against them, as though——

She closed her lips together violently, repudiating the dangerous thoughts sliding serpent-like into her consciousness.

Didn't she have enough to occupy her thoughts? she demanded scornfully of herself. Was she really so bereft of things to occupy herself that she had to fall into the kind of trap most women left behind them when they left behind their teens?

What was the purpose of daydreaming idiotic sensual fantasies about a man like Robert?

But he had touched her...had kissed her...

She made an impatient physical gesture with her arm as though trying to push away the emotional miasma, cutting her off from what she knew to be reality. This was the danger of never having allowed herself to make an emotional or physical commitment with another man. A part of her was still caught in the trap of the past; a part of her in some dangerous way was still intensely vulnerable to the emotions of that past.

No woman ever forgot her first lover. How could she, whatever the experience? But to cling so self-destructively to his memory, to refuse to allow herself the experience of any other memories with which to distance herself from him and to put their relationship in its proper perspective, surely that was taking self-immolation too far.

What was she trying to do? Punish herself because of Robert's lack of love for her, make herself feel that she was unworthy, unfit...unable to be loved? And by whom? By *any* man at all or just by Robert?

It wasn't like that; she wasn't a fool, wallowing in self-inflicted torment and misery—she was mature and sensible. So sensible that she had actually allowed Robert to touch her, to kiss her? That was sensible, was it? Her face twisted. Sensible would have been to have told him to leave...or even better never to have opened the door to him in the first place. Forget his motives, dubious though they must be; it was time to think of her own, to ask herself coldly and clinically just why she could not put the past behind her and forget it.

Another man—another lover might have helped the healing process, but she had never allowed that man, that lover the opportunity to make contact with her. Instead she had clung to her memories, her misery...her tormenting self-doubts and guilts.

Perhaps the only way she could overcome them was to confront them, to allow herself to—to what? To be touched...to be kissed...to be used.

What was the matter with her? Did she actually want to go back to the misery and pain of loving him? No, of course she didn't. She wasn't that kind of woman. Was she?

CHAPTER FIVE

'HAVE you lost weight?'

Elaine's accusing question made Holly sigh a little as she fibbed, 'No, I don't think so. Did you have a good journey?'

'You know British Rail,' Elaine responded wryly. 'Although I have to admit they do their best; instead of leaving everyone in silence and ignorance when the train stops for no apparent reason, they give you a second-by-second description of *why* nothing is happening. I don't know which experience is the more infuriating,' she added with a grin.

Both of them laughed.

'Thanks for coming to pick me up, by the way. I'm sorry to land myself on you at such short notice, but it seemed too good an opportunity to miss. One of the things I wanted to discuss with you was a link-up between you and another of our clients—a young designer who's basing her collection on the use of natural and, where possible, recycled materials. I've seen some of her stuff, and I thought what an impact it could make if we combined a photograph of you wearing some of her designs with the launch of the new perfume, focusing heavily on the natural, environmental-friendly aspect of both of you.'

Holly pulled a face.

'OK, OK, I know...but think about it,' Elaine suggested, as she followed Holly out of the hotel foyer and into the car park.

'I mean, from the media point of view it's a terrifically newsworthy angle. She's designed this suit from natural unbleached wool, and over it she drapes a length of tartan, a genuine plaid that she bought at a flea market. The effect is stunning——'

'She needn't have bothered buying one,' Holly interrupted her drily. 'I think we've still got the tartan blanket that used to go in the dog's basket, complete with authentic dog hairs.'

Elaine paused and looked at her.

'You really don't like the idea?'

'You know how I feel about being photographed and used as media hype,' Holly told her evasively, seeing her disappointment. 'If there were some way you could use her stuff without my having to wear it...'

'Well, I suppose we could try, but it wouldn't be anything like as effective. Where are we going, by the way?' she asked as Holly started the car. 'We could have eaten at the hotel.'

'I thought you might like to try this new wine-bar-cum-restaurant that's opened locally. It's very good. The food's very simple, very plain, very...'

'Organic and healthy?' Elaine supplied for her. 'OK. I give in.'

'It's housed in a medieval barn, with the kitchens open to view,' Holly told her, ignoring her comment. 'There's just something about it. I thought it might make a good background for the advertising campaign for the perfume.'

'I thought we'd already decided on some outdoorsy shots in Wales, all damp hillsides and mists.'

'Mmm . . . but the perfume is a winter scent; this place had open fires, exposed beams, a natural roughness that somehow blends in with all that I want the perfume to convey.'

'You mean, instead of suggesting that it will make the wearer smell of wet sheep, it will suggest they smell of damp wood,' Elaine teased her, immediately apologising, but Holly had a good sense of humour and couldn't help laughing, even while she was defending her new product.

It wasn't far to the restaurant. They parked outside in the gravelled car park. The floodlights used stored natural daylight as a light source, Holly explained to Elaine as they picked their way across the car park, and the gravel was being recycled, having been taken from a silted-up gravel pit locally which had now been turned into a lake.

'Recycled or not, it's still ruining my heels,' Elaine grumbled, although Holly noticed that she stopped grumbling the moment they stepped inside the barn, falling silent as she stared around at her surroundings.

'You're right,' she agreed after a few seconds. 'It *is* different. And do you know, I think you could be right...about using it in the ad campaign. Would the owners be agreeable, do you think?'

'I don't know. I haven't got that far. I'm not sure who the owners actually are. I do know the chef. He's a local lad who's been backed by someone—I'm not sure who.

'Would you like a drink or shall we go straight to our table?' she asked Elaine.

'Oh, let's eat. I'm starving and, besides, we can talk more comfortably across a table.'

A smiling waiter showed them to their table, handing them their menus and then leaving them to study them.

'I was thinking,' Elaine began once they had ordered. 'It might be a good idea if you could come up to London for a few days. You'll need extra clothes for the launch and——'

'I'm not sure if I can,' Holly interrupted her. 'With Paul away——'

'Oh, but he'll be back before the launch, won't he?'

'Yes,' Holly agreed reluctantly. 'But I'm still not sure ...'

'Well, we can afford to leave it for a little while——' Elaine broke off as their food arrived, sampling her meal and then saying approvingly, 'Mm ... very nice. Your chef certainly knows his stuff.'

'He isn't *my* chef,' Holly told her drily.

'My goodness, *he's* attractive,' Elaine commented, staring discreetly over Holly's shoulder in the direction of the entrance. 'And he's on his own. Wow, that's what I call a man.'

'Sexist,' Holly chided her.

'Don't turn round now,' Elaine warned her. 'He's looking right at us. Or rather right at you. Just my luck. Heavens, he's coming over!'

Warned by some sixth sense, Holly tensed, abruptly jerking round just in time to see Robert less than three feet away from them and quite obviously heading for their table.

'Holly...I thought it was you.'

'Robert...' He had reached them now and she had no alternative but to introduce him to Elaine, who seemed not to pick up on the silent message she was trying to give her that she wanted Robert's stay to be as brief as possible and was instead flirting quite outrageously with him, ignoring her meal in favour of engaging him in conversation.

To her relief Holly heard Robert saying with concern, 'I'm keeping you from your meal. I'd better——'

'No, no of course you aren't. We were just between courses and I feel so full I'd prefer to wait a little while before tackling my main meal,' Elaine corrected him outrageously, patting her flat stomach and giving him a wide-eyed look as she drew her attention to her slender body.

'Are you waiting for friends?' she heard Elaine asking.

'No, I'm dining here alone this evening. A friend recommended this place and I thought I'd give it a try.'

'Alone? What a shame, you could have joined us, couldn't he, Holly?'

What could she say? She summoned a sick grimace and pointed out as airily as she could, 'We're halfway through our meal and——'

'Oh, I don't mind waiting for my main course,' Elaine interrupted her, adding coyly, 'Unless of course you prefer to eat alone, Robert...'

Holly waited, her stomach muscles tensing as she prayed that he would ignore Elaine's light-hearted flirtation and walk away, but to her dismay he said easily, 'Hardly. I'd be delighted to join you.'

As though by magic a waiter appeared, and then so did another place-setting and another chair and Robert solved the problem of delaying the serving of their main meal by announcing that he would forgo a starter so that they could all eat together.

Ten minutes later, stoically trying to force down the food she no longer wanted, Holly listened in an increasingly brooding and resentful silence as Elaine expertly flattered and questioned Robert.

'So you're now basing your business in this country. Won't that be a tremendous adjustment to make after New York?'

'Not really. I've been planning to come back for a long time.'

Holly's hand faltered, her fork halfway to her mouth, her expression betraying her surprise. But then why should she be surprised? Just because she had assumed when he left that he had gone for good? Just as she had not known about his desire to own the Hall, so he might have kept other plans, other ambitions from her. After all, why should he ever have wanted to share them with her? She had meant nothing to him...nothing at all.

The tears that suddenly stung her eyes took her off guard. She put down her fork, blinking rapidly, quickly turning her head away from him, praying that he wouldn't have seen the betraying sheen in her eyes.

She could sense him turning his head in her direction. Panic overwhelmed her. She blinked frantically.

By now Elaine had noticed her distress and to forestall the anxious question she could see she was about to ask Holly told her huskily, 'It's all right...it's just an eyelash. It's gone now.'

'They're a nuisance, aren't they?' Elaine said sympathetically, dropping her flirtatious bantering with Robert to commiserate with her. 'I've lost count of the number of times one has ruined my carefully applied eye make-up.'

As she delved in her handbag for a handkerchief, quickly blowing her nose, Holly heard Robert saying, 'I'm glad I've bumped into you like this, Holly. I wanted to fix a firm date for you to come over and see the garden.'

With Elaine listening and watching with curious expectancy, Holly felt obliged to explain to her that Robert wanted her advice on the replanning of his garden, which of course led on to a discussion about the house itself.

'It sounds fantastic,' Elaine enthused. 'Just the kind of place we're looking for as a background for the magazine ads for Holly's new perfume, isn't it, Holly?'

'I thought you'd already decided that this place was ideal for that purpose,' Holly reminded her. Was Elaine seriously trying to attract Robert's attention? She had initially thought that the other woman was simply engaging in a little light-hearted flirting that meant nothing, but now, abruptly and painfully, she wasn't quite so sure.

The sharp shift in her emotions from acceptance to resentment startled her. She liked Elaine and had always got on well with her, but now suddenly she found herself almost on the verge of disliking her.

'There's no reason why we shouldn't use more than one background,' Elaine told her easily.

'I'm afraid the house is in no condition to be photographed at present. Parts of it aren't even safe,' Robert intervened.

'But you're living there...'

'I'm living in a cottage in the grounds,' he corrected her, 'and very basic the accommodation is, too, but I want to be on hand when the contractors start work.'

'Do you intend to use the place as a workplace as well as your home?' Elaine was asking him.

'Yes, that's the plan. I'm cutting down on my client base, so that I can handle the workload with a couple of PAs and a secretary. As I discovered when I was living in New York, there's far more to life than making money, although you don't always realise it until it's too late.'

'No, most successful men don't seem to be able to cut back on their work until they're forced to do so for health reasons,' Elaine agreed, adding, 'I must say I do admire you. I don't know if I'd have the moral fibre to give up a fast-track New York life to come back to Britain and live out in the country.'

While Holly looked on in a mixture of outrage and anger at Elaine's blatant flattery, Robert seemed impervious to it all, shrugging his shoulders and commenting only, 'I'd always intended to come back here, but there were ... reasons why it was impossible for me to make such a move earlier.'

Reasons ... Did he mean there had been a woman—a special woman who had kept him in New York? If so, why wasn't she here with him now? Who was she? What did she do? What was more important to her than being with Robert? While her imagination seethed with questions and their answers, she momentarily lost track of the conversation.

'Holly ... come back.'

The unexpected sensation of Robert touching her arm jerked her back to reality, her eyes widening as she instinctively drew back from him.

She was wearing a simple and very plain evening dress, but her arms were bare, and just for a second the touch of his fingers against her skin had reactivated her senses to such an extent that her body had almost mistaken his touch for a caress ... and, even worse, had virtually responded to it as a caress, so that in pulling away from him she was behaving in direct contradiction to the way her senses wanted her to behave. They wanted her not to pull away but to move closer to him, to invite a more sensual, slower, more deliberate caress ... the kind of caress which in the past might have been the prelude to their lovemaking.

'Poor Holly, you *were* miles away, weren't you?' Elaine teased her. 'What were you thinking about? The new perfume?'

'Or a certain medical administrator?' Robert suggested cynically.

Uncomfortably aware of Elaine's speculative look, Holly shook her head and told them, 'Neither, as it happens. Paul rang this afternoon. He's hoping to get back soon.'

As she had hoped, the introduction of her brother's name changed the focus of the conversation, Elaine announcing once again that she hoped that Paul had not forgotten his obligations to the launch of the new perfume.

'No, he'll be back well in time for that,' Holly assured her. They had all finished eating now and she ached to be free of the tension of Robert's presence. She didn't know which was worse, sitting here next to him, dreading doing or saying something which might focus his attention on her, or sitting here listening to Elaine flirting with him.

'I don't want to rush you, Elaine,' she said now. 'But you did say you were booked on an early train in the morning ...'

'Yes, I know. There are still some things we need to discuss, but we can do that back at the hotel, if you don't mind.'

Shaking her head, Holly started to push back her chair but almost immediately Robert stopped her.

'We still haven't fixed a date for you to come and look over the garden,' he reminded her. 'I was wondering if you might be free on Saturday?'

She ached to be able to refuse but she had never been the least adept at lying and so, instead of inventing some fictitious engagement which would have enabled her to reject his suggestion, she found that she was saying uncertainly, 'I really think it might be best if, as Angela suggested, you approached the professionals——'

'Oh, no, Holly,' Elaine interrupted her, telling Robert, 'You mustn't listen to her. She really is far too modest; her garden at the farm is wonderful.'

Her heart sinking, Holly acknowledged that there really was no way she could escape now without being openly aggressive and offensive.

Forcing a wan smile, she responded unenthusiastically, 'Well, if you're sure...'

'I'm sure,' Robert confirmed, getting up to stand beside her and help her out of her chair before performing the same polite office for Elaine.

Later, as Holly drove Elaine back to her hotel, the latter commented, 'That Robert really is something, isn't he? I didn't think men like him existed any more...masculine, sexy, successful—and single. Mm...I'd even bet that he's fantastic in bed as well—the kind of man who enjoys giving a woman pleasure.'

Holly couldn't help it. She could feel first her face and then her body starting to burn, and was thankful that the dark interior of the car prevented Elaine from seeing her.

'No comment?' Elaine questioned her, surprising her.

She shrugged her shoulders. 'Should there be?'

'Perhaps not, but I couldn't help noticing that, for all my determined and over-the-top efforts to flirt with him, *you* were the one he was interested in.'

'No!' The panic in the denial reached even her own ears, warning her that she was over-reacting. 'That is, I'm sure you're wrong. I've known him forever. He and Paul were schoolfriends.'

'So, that doesn't stop him fancying you, does it?'

'You're imagining things,' Holly told her flatly.

'If you say so,' Elaine concurred cheerfully, changing back to demand, 'Who's this medical administrator, by the way?'

By the time Holly had explained her relationship with John, they had reached the hotel.

It was another two hours before they had gone through all the points Elaine had wanted to raise.

Tired, Holly left her and made her way back to the car. If only they hadn't bumped into Robert tonight and if only she had not been stupid enough to agree to look over his garden. Had it been anyone but Robert who had asked for her help, she would have been interested as well as flattered. The restoration of old gardens was a subject which fascinated her.

She had no idea why Robert was being so insistent about her viewing the garden. After all, he could hardly want her company, and as for her opinions... So what was he doing? What was his purpose in insisting on seeing her?

'He fancies you,' Elaine had teased her. If only she knew just how wrong she was. Smothering a bitter smile, Holly turned into her own drive. When she got in she was going straight to bed, she promised herself, and in the morning she was most definitely not going to oversleep.

Neither was she going to waste her time in pointless dreams and memories of how it had felt to be held in Robert's arms; to lie against him, skin to skin, to touch and caress him with all the awkward shyness and ardour of a young girl with her first lover, to pour out on him all her yearning adoration and love.

She was trembling when she went inside, locking the door with unsteady fingers and then leaning on it while tears burned under her tightly closed eyelids. What was she doing to herself? Had she no sense, no pride? Oh, God, why did he have to come back and disrupt her life like this?

CHAPTER SIX

FOR the rest of the week, Holly tried to put Saturday and her agreement to look over Robert's gardens out of her mind. It should have been easy; her workload had increased while Paul was away and the launch of the new perfume range was putting added pressure on her, but somehow Robert still managed to creep into her thoughts, his presence there taking her unawares, making her tense her body as though in physical rejection of his mental image.

On Friday evening, she could not settle to anything, her glance constantly drawn to the telephone in her sitting-room.

She was overwhelmingly tempted to telephone Robert and tell him that she had changed her mind, but what if he insisted on making another date? There was, after all, no way she could let down her guard and tell him openly and honestly that she could not afford to allow her vulnerable senses any kind of contact with him.

There was a pile of books on the coffee-table—gardening books which she had extracted from her collection with the purpose of refreshing her memory on the type of gardens which would originally have been laid out around a house such as the Hall.

Had the inhabitants been wealthy enough, there would have been sophisticated walkways, arbours and formal beds surrounded by immaculate hedges or walls—gardens where the ladies of the house could walk in peace and privacy. There might even have been an early variation of a tennis court, and there would certainly have been a well-established kitchen garden.

It was only later that such formality had given way to the parkland of the Georgian and Regency eras. For the Stuarts and their courtiers the Dutch had been a strong source of inspiration, and Holly had a very expensive book which Paul had bought her the previous Christmas with some beautiful illustrations taken from paintings depicting these formal Dutch gardens with their topiary and formal beds, their long, straight canals and symmetrically shaped pools. She picked up the book, opening it, frowning over it, trying to force herself to concentrate on it. Beside her she had a notepad and a pen, supposedly to jot down anything which she thought might be useful, but so far all she had written was, 'Hall Garden'.

At eleven o'clock, she acknowledged defeat and went to bed. It was only one day, a few short hours and then, like a nasty dose of medicine, it would be over, and she would be safe, she comforted herself as she lay in bed. And after all, what was there to fear? She knew the dangers—knew them and would be on her guard against them, wouldn't she?

*   *   *

She woke up early with the warning signs of a tension headache building up behind her eyes. Outside the sun was shining and the blue sky held all the promise of a warm sunny day.

She dressed accordingly, donning jeans and a T-shirt, catching her hair up on top of her head in a pony-tail so that it would be out of the way, leaving her skin free of anything other than some protective moisturiser and a touch of lip-gloss to protect her lips.

No way was Robert going to be allowed to think that she cared enough about his opinion to don flattering clothes and make-up for him.

Downstairs she made some coffee and had her cereal. The papers had arrived along with the post, and while she opened her mail she read quickly through the headlines.

She was just wrapping some of her reference books in protective cling-film, prior to taking them out to the car, when she heard a vehicle drawing up outside.

Frowning, she went to the sitting-room window. A large Range Rover was parked outside. Her frown deepened. She knew of no one owning such a vehicle who was likely to visit her at this time of the morning.

But before she could turn away to go and open the door she saw Robert alighting from the vehicle. He stopped, catching sight of her standing there. Like her, he was dressed in worn jeans, a checked shirt tucked in at the waist, the sleeves rolled back to reveal his forearms.

He looked for all the world as though he had spent his entire life living here in the country, she reflected, as he smiled at her and waved. Her heart was hammering heavily against her ribs, the tension in her muscles making her head pound.

When she unlocked the front door and released the safety-chain, her fingers felt cold and stiff.

'Hi. I thought I'd come round and pick you up, save you driving over...'

He was inside the house now, sniffing appreciatively as he commented, 'Mm...freshly brewed coffee. It smells wonderful.'

Holly compressed her lips.

'I was just finishing my breakfast,' she told him curtly. She wasn't going to offer him any coffee. She wasn't going to do or say anything that would encourage him to think—to think what? That she still wanted him, still ached for him...still loved him?

As she turned her back on him, leaving him standing in the hall, she hurried into the kitchen, but, to her shock, instead of staying where he was he followed her, glancing assessingly round the room and then saying admiringly, 'Now this is how a kitchen should look. Who planned and designed it for you?'

'No one,' Holly told him stiffly. 'I did it myself.'

There was a small pause and then he said softly, 'Yes, of course, I should have guessed, shouldn't I? You always did believe that the kitchen was the heart of a home. I remember how you used to tell me that when you got married you wanted a big kitchen with the kind of table the whole family could sit round. I seem to remember in those days that you wanted four children...'

Holly could feel the wave of burning scarlet moving up over her body in a painful, stinging tide.

'We all tend to have unrealistic and idealistic dreams when we're that age,' she managed to retort as she turned her back on him.

'Idealistic maybe...but surely not unrealistic. You haven't married—but then these days a woman doesn't need a husband to be a mother, does she?'

Keeping her back to him, Holly reached for her coffee-mug, but her hand was trembling so much that some of the hot liquid jerked out over the rim, splashing down on to her jeans.

Instantly Robert was at her side, exclaiming over the accident, demanding to know if she was hurt. Frantically trying to keep some distance between them, Holly scrubbed at the small damp patch on her jeans, shaking her head, her throat too constricted with tension for her to be able to speak.

'Here, you'd better let me do that,' Robert told her, taking the cloth she had snatched up from her hand, adding, 'You're trembling like a leaf. Are you sure you're all right?'

'I'm fine. It was just the shock,' Holly lied. It was true that she was shocked, but that shock hadn't been caused by the unexpected heat of the hot coffee against her skin. No, Robert was the one who was causing her to tremble so badly. She ached for him to move away from her, panic surging over her as he pressed the cloth to her damp jeans.

'It's all right...I can manage,' she told him, pulling quickly away from him. 'I'll have to go and change my jeans, though.'

'Any chance of some of that coffee while I'm waiting?' he asked her.

What could she say? He could see for himself that the filter-jug was half full. To refuse would not just be churlish, it would be bad-mannered as well.

'Help yourself,' she told him in a stilted voice. 'I shan't be long.'

Upstairs, she wrenched off her jeans, briefly examining the small scarlet patch on her thigh. The scald was only minor, nothing at all really, and if the truth were known she could feel the imprint of Robert's fingers against her skin where he had held her as he mopped up the coffee far more intensely than she could feel any burning sensation from the liquid.

It only took her seconds to collect a clean pair of jeans, but to put them on took much longer, principally because she was still trembling violently, her senses relaying to her over and over again all the unwanted information they had gathered in those few seconds while Robert had bent over her. She could still smell the scent of his skin, feel the faint roughness of the pads of his fingertips, and if she closed her eyes she could even hear the sound of his breathing and see the familiar outline of his jaw, remembering how eagerly a lifetime ago she had pressed her immature and inexperienced lips to it, tasting his skin, shocked by his response at the time as she thrilled to the knowledge that her touch excited him. How easily and how treacherously her lips could recall the slightly rough sensation of his skin, the sensual pleasure of that delicate friction against the sensitivity of her mouth; the way he had moved, so that she could explore the lean column of his throat, the way his hands had tightened around her waist as he pulled her closer to him, so close in fact that she could feel the hard throb of his body.

She was trembling so much now that she could barely fasten her jeans, her fingers almost numb with shocked reaction to her erotic thoughts—thoughts she had no right to have, thoughts she did not want to have. She swallowed a hysterical sob of frightened anger. Why did he have to come back? Why couldn't he have stayed safely away and, once having returned, why did he have to seek her out like this...tormenting her...reminding her? Yes, it was true that once she had shyly and innocently confided to him her dreams: dreams of a husband, a lover, and the life she would live with him, a life which had included children, a life which would have allowed her to give full rein to her yearning to recreate for those children the same family atmosphere and security she herself had known. Was that so very wrong? She had, after all, been young...and immature, perhaps, for her age. Was it *her* fault that she had believed he loved her, that she had confused sexual desire with emotional need...that she had believed that their futures lay together?

Holly stared blindly out of her bedroom window, wishing he had not reminded her of those dreams, wishing he had not so cruelly pointed out to her

that, while she might have realised her dream of a
home that was comfortable and welcoming, she did
not have the husband she had longed for, nor the
children he would have given her. And yet she was
content . . . more than content, and she had learned
enough now to know that a woman could have a
fulfilled and very happy life without a man in it.
When she looked at other people's relationships she
saw that they were often flawed, that they were not
perfection. And besides, she *could* have married,
had she chosen to do so. The fact was that she had
never been able to bring herself to take the risk of
falling in love a second time—and without
love . . . without love there was no point in marrying. At least not to her . . .

She had considered her life fulfilled and happy,
and yet with those few brief words Robert had
somehow made it seem as though she had been
forced to accept second best—as though she had
had to settle for less than her ideal. And yet that
was not the case.

All right, so it was true that her life had taken a
very different direction from that she had envisaged at eighteen, but could she honestly say now
that even if she had married, even if she had had
children that she would not have wanted and needed
more, that there would not have come a time when
intellectually, when perhaps selfishly, she would
have needed to achieve something for herself,
something outside her home and family, something
which belonged to her and her alone?

The sound of the kitchen door opening made her
tense.

'Holly, are you OK?'

Robert was standing in the hall. If he came upstairs looking for her... Hurriedly she finished dressing, calling out to him, 'Yes, I'm fine,' as she opened her bedroom door and hurried along the landing.

As she turned the corner of the stairs she saw that he was standing at the bottom, one hand on the newel post as he looked upwards. For a moment she faltered. He looked so very masculine, so heart-shakingly familiar. It would be the easiest thing in the world to run down to him, to fling herself into his arms, to tell him how she missed him, to beg him to hold her and never let her go.

Horrified, she averted her face from him, praying that he would move out of the way before she reached the bottom stair, and yet when he did the surge of disappointment that swept her taunted her, mercilessly revealing her own weakness.

'I've just got some books to collect,' she told him as she hurried past him.

When she returned with them he was still standing in the hall.

'I've emptied the coffee-filter and washed up,' he told her.

She gave him a startled look. She hadn't imagined a man in his position would have given a thought to such mundane domestic trivia.

Once they were outside he took the books from her, unlocking the passenger door of the Range Rover and helping her inside, before opening the back door and depositing the books on the rear seat.

He had always been a good driver, skilled but aware of the deficiencies of others and the hazards that could occur. Once she had loved nothing better than to sit beside him in the old sports car he had rebuilt, but now she discovered that she was keeping herself as far away from him as she could, concentrating on the view outside her window as though it were completely unfamiliar to her instead of something she saw every day.

They were almost halfway to the Hall, when he shocked her by asking, 'Why *have* you never married, Holly?'

How could he of all people dare to ask her that? Did he really not know what he had done to her? How much he had hurt her? Was he really trying to pretend that he hadn't *known* that when she'd talked of marriage what she had wanted had been marriage to *him* ... ?

As her body tensed in self-defence, the need to protect herself made her respond with a vehemence that was almost aggressive.

'I don't really see that's any concern of yours, Robert, but, if you must know, what I've seen of other people's marriages hasn't inclined me to make that kind of commitment. For every couple I know who are genuinely happily married, there seem to be two or three other couples who merely endure one another, who exist in mutual apathy and sometimes in mutual dislike.'

'You don't think that perhaps you're taking a negative and biased view of marriage?' he suggested quietly. 'After all, no one really knows what goes on inside a relationship apart from the two

people themselves. What can seem an unsatis-
factory partnership to the onlooker might suit the
couple involved very well. After all, these couples
you mentioned whose relationships seem to be less
than idealistic *are* still together, aren't they?

'Nothing to say?' he probed when she made no
response.

'What *can* I say?' Holly demanded. 'Other than
that, I'm astonished to hear you of all men defending the married state.'

She didn't bother to conceal either her bitterness
or her contempt. Her throat felt raw as though she
had been crying for hours and she was conscious
of a sick shakiness weakening her body. What was
the matter with her? *Why* was she allowing him to
do this to her... to upset her so much? What did
it matter to her how much his views had changed?
He meant nothing to her now, nothing at all.

'Tell me something, Holly,' she heard him saying
gravely. 'Am I to be everlastingly punished and
condemned for the sins and omissions of an immature and, dare I admit it, aggressively misguided
twenty-two-year-old, who was too arrogant and too
blind to recognise what he had? Yes, I was over-
ambitious, and, yes, I did have my values the wrong
way round, but I like to think that I've moved on
a good bit from that boy I was then to the man I
am now. I'm not saying that some of that learning
process hasn't been painful to others as well as to
me, but I *have* learned, Holly. Why do you think
I've come back here?'

She had started to shake inside. She felt sick with
anger and distrust. Was he really trying to pretend

that he had come back because of her...that he regretted the way he had hurt her, the way he had left her?

'I really don't know,' she told him tightly, 'and neither do I care. As far as I'm concerned the past is over...dead...finished. You say you've changed—well, so have I. I'm not the girl I was at eighteen, Robert, and I certainly don't regret that change. And if you're imagining that I haven't married because—because of what happened between us...' She was shaking so much, she could hardly speak, but the words had to be said; out of pride if nothing else she could not, would not allow him to think that her single state had anything to do with him. 'Well, you're wrong. There have been other men in my life, you know.'

'Yes, I'm sure there have,' he agreed, but his voice was terse and when she risked darting a brief glance at him he was staring straight ahead, his jaw tight and hard.

The panic she had been trying to suppress all week bubbled over inside her. She was just about to tell him that she had changed her mind, that if he needed advice about his garden then he must get it from someone else, when he turned into the Hall's drive.

'Strange the way things work out, isn't it?' he commented curtly. 'Here I am, back in the village which in my arrogance I thought was too small, too parochial for me, wanting nothing more than to settle down and raise my family here, while you, the one who claimed to want only the love of a husband and children, have become a successful and innovative businesswoman who apparently has no time in her life for any kind of permanent commitment other than to her career.'

Holly's throat was too constricted for her to speak. She ached to be able to give way to her emotions, to turn to Robert and to scream at him that *he* was the reason she had devoted herself to her business, that it was because of *him* that she was too afraid to let herself love again...that it was because of *him* that she distrusted her own judgement so much that she dared not allow herself to believe that a man could love her, could want her.

How dared he come back here now and casually tell her that he had changed, that he had learned, that he now wanted all those things he had so fiercely repudiated before? Or had it just been *her* whom he had repudiated? She smiled bitterly to herself, imagining the kind of woman he would now marry, someone sleek and cool...a woman who would grace the home he would give her, a woman who would give him one or perhaps two perfect children, a woman whom he could wear on his arm like a prize. Not her kind of woman. The partner, the lover Holly wanted now was a man who would share his life with her, who would encourage her independence and her achievements, a man who would take real pride and pleasure in her success instead of simply seeing her as an accompaniment to his own.

What Robert no doubt wanted was a younger Angela. Robert had stopped the car. Immediately she opened the door, jumping out quickly before he could come round to help her, before he could touch her.

'I thought we'd have a coffee before we start,' he told her after giving her a thoughtful look.

She wanted to refuse, but her senses warned her that, like a hunting animal with its prey, he would quickly sense her vulnerability and take advantage of it. What did he really want of her? she wondered sickly as she nodded her head and followed him towards the main house.

Surely he hadn't been implying that he wanted to reactivate their old relationship? No, he couldn't have been. Perhaps, then, he had simply been warning her that he was here to stay and that she must accustom herself both to that fact and the fact that he intended to marry—someone else. But why bother? After all, there must have been other women in his life since her, and she had never meant anything to him in the first place.

Sick and confused, Holly barely gave the huge, dismal kitchen a glance as he led the way into it.

'It's not a patch on yours, I know,' he was telling her. 'In fact I could do with a woman's advice when it comes to re-designing it.'

'Ask Angela. I'm sure she'll be delighted to help you,' Holly told him tersely.

'Yes. I'm sure she will,' he agreed.

He was watching her. She could feel it, but she refused to turn round and look at him.

'Holly...'

His voice was unexpectedly gentle, tender almost. She could feel the hot rush of tears stabbing her eyes, the aching misery of the pain that flared inside her as she fought down her longing to run to him, to have his arms open to hold her, to have his mouth on hers.

What was wrong with her? She mustn't feel like this. It was treachery to her own principles, the destruction of all she had fought to gain.

Why was she being so weak, so stupid, why was she allowing herself to fall into the same old trap? Hadn't she learned *anything*, anything at all from the past?

'Don't bother with any coffee for me,' she told him brusquely. 'I'll go and wait outside for you while you have yours. Oh, by the way, do you have any plans or drawings of the gardens?'

'I don't know. There's a huge pile of stuff in the library, but I haven't had time to go through it yet. Some of it is so badly mildewed and damaged that it will probably have to be thrown out. I did get a pile of deeds and other stuff when I bought the place. There could be something among that lot.'

His voice sounded flat and tired, defeated almost. Had she misread the situation? Could he genuinely have regretted the past? Could he . . . ?

Bitterly she squashed the hope beginning to flare inside her. What was she doing? He had told her once that he didn't love her; she surely wasn't going to allow him to do the same thing to her again . . .

Quickly she opened the door and hurried through the maze of larders and store-rooms until she found the door into the stable yard. Once there, she stood still breathing deeply, trying to calm her inner tremors.

Why on earth had she ever agreed to come here today? And why on earth was she still so vulnerable to him? She hated herself for that—for still being weak and stupid enough to be swayed by his apparent desire to reach out to her...to apologise for the past.

She was standing with her body hunched, staring into space when she heard the door open.

'It's this way,' she heard him saying to her, and she stiffened as he touched her arm lightly, wheeling away from him to keep as much distance between them as she could as he indicated a wooden door in the peripheral wall.

The door led into a traditional kitchen garden, now a riot of weeds and overgrown fruit bushes and trees—a veritable wilderness, Holly recognised as she studied it in silence.

'If you intend to have a kitchen garden,' she told him quietly, 'all of this will have to be cleared. Some of the espaliered fruit trees could be retained, and it will require the attention of a full-time gardener. It will be a very expensive way of producing your own vegetables and fruit, but having said that——'

'Having said that, there will be the advantage of knowing my family is eating healthy organically grown food.'

Holly shrugged, trying not to react to that emotive word 'family'.

'You can buy organically grown stuff at the local supermarket these days far more cheaply.'

'All right, let's say, then, for argument's sake that I want to retain the kitchen garden and that I can afford the costs involved. How long would it take to get it back in order?'

'That depends on who you get to do the work and how many men they can spare. That and how skilled and experienced they are, but at a guess if you started now and if you were very, very lucky, and the weather was with you, you could have your first crops planted by next spring.'

'Mm ... Any suggestions as to who might do the job?'

Holly shrugged. 'It depends on exactly what you want, and how much you're prepared to pay.'

'Mm ... well, that's something we can discuss when you've seen the rest of the garden.'

Two hours later, hot and sticky from the sun, and longing for a cool drink, Holly could only marvel at both Robert's stamina and his ability to remain cool and fresh when she felt anything but.

The gardens were far more extensive than she had expected and very, very neglected, but once long ago someone had cherished and cared for them, and, as she had pointed out to Robert with envy, the long borders protected by high yew hedges that separated the formal area of the gardens from the more informal, once restored, would be breathtakingly magnificent.

At one end of them, a flight of steps led to an enclosed area of formal flower-beds and another walled garden, at the other the vista opened out to reveal a large circular pond, cherubs holding dolphins that spouted water into it. Beneath the canopy of huge lily leaves, Holly glimpsed the orange backs of some huge goldfish.

Beyond the pond lay a lawn, a stone porticoed summer-house facing the pond and flanked on either side with a stone-columned pergola. Once roses had probably adorned the columns, but now they, like the overhead struts, had disappeared.

As they made their way through the weed-infested lawn, Holly paused to admire the lines of the summer-house, impulsively stepping forward to go into it.

'No!'

The sharp command in Robert's voice made her stiffen and turn round just as his hand grasped her upper arm, his fingers biting painfully into her flesh.

'The roof isn't safe,' he told her, and as she glanced upwards she saw that there was a huge crack running across one of the stone ceiling segments.

'I should have warned you before,' she heard Robert saying as she stared sickly at the huge slab of stone poised so precariously.

She was shivering despite the heat of the sun, feeling both sick and oddly light-headed.

'Look, I think you'd better sit down.'

She could tell that he was frowning without having to look at him. What a fool he must think her, but it wasn't so much the shock of the near accident that might have befallen her that was making her feel so weak as the fact that he was still holding on to her. He had moved somehow so that he was standing behind her. She could feel the heat of his body; she felt totally engulfed by him...weak and vulnerable.

'There's a bench over there,' he told her, indicating a stone seat almost overgrown by grass. 'You go and sit down for a few minutes. If you'll excuse me, there's something I have to do.'

Only too glad to be released from her physical and mental bondage to him, Holly stepped away from Robert, and walked shakily over to the seat he had indicated. By the time she turned round he had gone and she was completely alone. Well, not completely, she realised, as she saw a rabbit, apparently oblivious to her presence, hopping across the grass, pausing every now and again to chew busily.

Given a good deal of time and even more money, these gardens could be breathtakingly beautiful, she reflected enviously as she closed her eyes and soaked up the heat of the sun. Already her imagination was painting them as they could be, imagining how they might look. They were large enough, too, to allow plenty of space for a play area for children, even for a cricket pitch and a tennis court, and in the paddock beyond the gardens there was plenty of space for a couple of fat, lazy ponies...

A sharp pain twisted inside her. What was she thinking... imagining? Once before she had allowed herself to daydream of having Robert's children, but then she had been a naïve, trusting fool, who had believed every word, every lie he had told her.

She closed her eyes, not so much against the heat of the sun but more against the press of hot tears that burned behind her eyelids. She hardly recognised herself any more, hardly knew what emotional folly she was likely to commit next.

'Holly, are you all right?'

The low-voiced question made her tense and open her eyes.

She hadn't heard Robert's soft-footed approach across the lawn. Now he was standing beside her, frowning down at her. He was, she noticed, carrying a blanket and a large picnic hamper.

'I—I'm fine,' she told him, instantly defensive and afraid, eyeing both him and what he was carrying suspiciously.

'Lunch,' he told her, smiling at her. 'I thought it would be more pleasant to eat it out here. The house is far from comfortable at the moment.' He added wryly, 'I suspect I'm going to be living in my cottage for a long time to come as well. The architects tell me it's going to take well into next year just to clear away the debris and start work on the renovations, and as for the trouble we've been having finding suitably skilled craftsmen...'

He put down the hamper, and then hunkered down on the grass, spreading the blanket. 'Come and sit down here,' he told her, patting it. 'It will be far more comfortable than that seat. Oh, and I've brought these as well.'

Wrapped in the blanket had been two huge cushions, which he now propped up against a tree-trunk.

'There was no need for you to go to so much trouble,' Holly told him grittily as he opened the hamper. 'We've almost finished. I could have gone home for lunch.'

'Yes, but don't you find that food is almost always more enjoyable when it's eaten in the company of someone else?' he asked her softly.

'That depends on who the someone else is,' Holly retorted bleakly, refusing to allow herself to acknowledge what she was beginning to feel.

She had started to stand up and now he came over to her, taking hold of her shoulders and holding her far too firmly for her to move away.

'Holly, can't we declare a truce?' he said quietly. 'I know I hurt you, I know I behaved badly, and I know as well that from your point of view my apology is all too probably far too little and far too late. You were always such a compassionate, loving girl; can't you find it in your heart to allow me the comfort of acknowledging how badly I treated you, of allowing me the make amends?'

'By doing what?' she demanded brittly. 'Asking my advice on your garden and feeding me lunch?'

Robert's mouth twitched as though he was about to laugh, and she was shocked by the thrust of sensation that pierced her, the desire to reach out and touch his mouth, to trace the well-remembered shape of his lips.

'Well, not really. *They* were both more for my benefit than yours. I'm not asking you to forgive me—why should you?'

'Then what are you asking?' she asked aggressively.

He gave her a sombre, brooding look, searching her face as though looking for something he had lost and desperately missed, and then he said slowly,

'Perhaps just the opportunity to prove to you that I *have* changed.'

'We've both changed, Robert,' she told him fiercely. 'I've changed too.'

'Yes,' he agreed. 'Yes, you have.' She tensed in his grip. 'You're a woman now, Holly, not a girl. Can't the woman in you find it in her heart to put aside the past and allow us to start again?'

'There's no reason for us to start again. No point. Nothing...'

'Yes, there is. There's this,' Robert corrected her, and as she looked questioningly up at him she knew that he was going to kiss her...knew it and did nothing to stop him, to evade or check him...simply standing there with the sun on her upturned face and her body trembling as though she were in the grip of a dangerous fever.

His hands against her face were sun-warm, and firm, his fingertips slightly rough as they smoothed her skin, his head blotting out the light, his eyes looking straight into hers.

He had always kissed her like this, with his eyes open, whispering to her to do the same. When she had protested he had told her roughly that he wanted to see what she was feeling when he kissed her...that he wanted to look deep into her heart and her soul and to know that she was sharing with him his desire...his love.

But now she kept her eyes open out of a need to protect herself, too afraid to close them in case she completely slipped away from reality to a place where she could only feel...a place where reason could not exist—a place from which the only exit was laced with pain and anguish. As she well knew . . .

'Holly.' He breathed her name against her lips as he whispered, 'There is still this, isn't there?' And then he was kissing her—no, not kissing her, what he was doing was subtly seducing her senses, by caressing her mouth with his, by stroking it over and over again with the warm pressure of his lips until hers softened and clung, until she was dizzy with the strength of the hot, aching pleasure that was beginning to burn through her.

His hands still cupped her face, holding her in gentle bondage, his fingers stroking her skin, seeking and finding the vulnerable places on her skull, the hollow behind her ears, the tender nape of her neck. A shudder tormented her, her mouth parting in an instinctive protest, and then too late she recognised that that unvoiced protest could all too easily have been interpreted as a plea for the increased pressure of his mouth, for the slow stroke of his tongue, for the sudden movement that brought his body into closer contact with hers.

The sound of denial and pain she made deep in her throat somehow become transmuted into one of need and longing. Robert's hands left her face to gather her body close to his, and weakly, stupidly, she let him, her flesh as soft and pliable as water-weed, allowing him to wrap her so closely to him that her heartbeat took its rhythm from his.

'Holly, Holly . . .'

Was he actually sighing her name or was it just the sound of the grass as it moved in the breeze?

She felt dizzy, disorientated and totally out of control.

It was that knowledge that tensed her, checking her response, turning her body's acceptance into rejection as she stiffened in Robert's arms, dragging her mouth away from his.

'Holly.'

'No... no. I don't want this,' she told him frantically, pulling away from him. 'Let me go, Robert. This isn't what I came here for—and if you think for one moment that I'd be stupid enough to let you use me now the way you did before... If you think——'

'You responded to me,' he told her softly. 'You——'

She had to stop this and now before it was too late and she was totally humiliated.

'I'm a woman, not a girl,' she interrupted him. 'Of course I responded to you... just as I would have responded to any attractive man in the same circumstances. We're both adults now, Robert. We both understand the force of sexual desire.'

She had to turn away from him in case he challenged her, in case he guessed that she was lying. She had never in her life responded to another man like this and she suspected that she never would. But sexual desire was all that it was. Her body had remembered that he had once been its lover and it had been to that memory, to the past, that it had responded—not the man he was now.

'I think it's time I went home,' she told him grittily. 'And if you really want my advice on your garden, then I suggest you do as Angela recommended and call in the experts. Or why not give Angela herself a call? I'm sure she'd be delighted to come round and—share your lunch.'

She had turned away from him and set off across the lawn before she remembered that she had no car, but as she hesitated he caught up with her and told her quietly, 'I'm sorry if I upset you. I only wanted——'

He stopped speaking and shook his head.

'It doesn't matter. I'll drive you home.' He saw her face and gave her a sardonic look. 'It's all right. You'll be perfectly safe. If that's what you want...'

Holly couldn't allow it to go unchallenged. She forced herself to give him a long, cool look.

'Yes, that *is* what I want,' she told him emphatically, and she told herself that it was true and that the sensations, the feeling, the desire and the urgency she had experienced in his arms had simply been by-products of the past... ancient echoes of something that was long dead and could safely be forgotten—that *had* to be forgotten.

She had no idea why Robert was pursuing her like this, or what he really wanted from her, but what she did know was that she didn't trust him, could not trust him; that it would be safer, wiser to make it plain to him right now that she did not want him in her life. After all, he wasn't going to have any problems finding someone who would be only too happy to——

To what? To become his lover? Was *that* what he had in mind for her? After all, he had lived in New York. He must have witnessed at first hand the effect of living promiscuously. Who safer to have sex with than the girl he had first known as a virgin? She smiled bitterly to herself. Even safer than he imagined, since there hadn't been anyone else since then.

CHAPTER SEVEN

HOLLY had a date that evening with John. She prepared for it reluctantly, chastising herself for her lack of enthusiasm. Had she wanted to marry, John would have made an ideal husband. He had already indicated that he could quite easily fall in love with her. He respected her, and he would never try to dominate her. He would be a devoted husband and father, and she suspected that he could quite possibly be an adoring and sensual lover. And so why, given that despite everything that she had said to Robert she did still want a family, even if she had buried that need away deep inside herself, why was she turning John away, rejecting him instead of encouraging him? Why, whenever he took her in his arms, did she freeze and turn her head away? Why, as with every other man she had dated, had she found herself totally unable to respond to him as a man?

Was it because Robert had hurt her, or was it because she was afraid that no other man could touch her emotions as he had done—that no other man could arouse and delight her... that no other man could ever take her to such exquisite heights of ecstasy? She gave a small shudder. Was that why this afternoon she had not resisted him sooner— why she had simply stood there while he had held her, touched her, kissed her?

125

Was she really so much of a fool?

She and John, together with three other couples, had been invited to dinner by one of John's colleagues, a senior surgeon at the hospital.

Holly had met their host and hostess before and vaguely knew the other guests, but she was rather disconcerted when they arrived at the large modern house on the outskirts of town to be treated as though she were some kind of celebrity.

Over dinner the male guests vied for her attention, complimenting her on her business skills.

'Most astute of you to have jumped so quickly on to this environmental bandwagon,' one of the men commented half enviously.

Holly compressed her lips, and told him coolly that, far from jumping on any bandwagons, she considered it every adult's duty and responsibility to protect the environment for those generations yet to come.

The man looked rather disconcerted and put out. He was somewhere in his mid-fifties, balding with a florid countenance and a waistline that looked as though it was a victim of too many stodgy business dinners. His wife was thin and slightly nervy. Holly saw her tense whenever he spoke, as though she was half afraid of him.

In contrast one of the other couples, who must have been about the same age, were completely different, both of them well-informed and open-minded. The wife had recently embarked on an adult university course, and kept them all amused by describing the traumas of going back to full-time education in the same classroom as teenagers.

'On the whole they're very tolerant,' she told them, 'and very kind.'

Holly and John were the first couple to leave, Holly explaining that she had an early start planned in the morning and that she intended to spend the day working in her garden.

Her head had begun to ache. She put it down to the red wine she had drunk with her meal. She felt on edge and tense, unable to relax properly. She told herself it was because of her irritation with Norman Simpson and his inability to accept that they all had a responsibility to do something positive towards protecting the environment, but she knew that the root cause of her malaise went much deeper than a surface irritation with a man too wilfully blind to accept that others were changing where he was not.

Guiltily aware that she had not been the best of companions, she invited John in for a nightcap, apologising for having dragged him away early.

'I was ready to leave myself,' he told her as he followed her into the kitchen.

She had just made them both mugs of coffee and sat down opposite him when he said gently, 'Something's wrong, Holly, and I think I can guess what, or rather who is causing it.'

She stared at him, and then shrugged.

'Oh, I know it was stupid to allow myself to get annoyed with Norman Simpson, but that kind of attitude——'

'I wasn't referring to Norman Simpson, idiot though he undoubtedly is. No, the problem goes much deeper than that, doesn't it? It's Robert, isn't it?'

Holly was too shocked and dismayed to conceal her reaction. She had never expected John to show such perception, such intuition.

Her eyes widened, the pupils darkening, the colour running up under her skin, betraying her even before she started to stammer.

'No—No...of course it isn't. Why should he——?'

'Holly, there's no need to pretend with me,' John told her gently. 'And even if if I hadn't heard on the grapevine that you and he were once very close, the way you reacted to the mention of his name just now...the way his presence affected you at the assembly rooms... Do you still love him?'

'No—no of course I don't,' Holly repudiated violently.

John gave her a thoughtful, almost sad look. She found that it was difficult for her to meet his eyes, that she was looking away from him almost as though she had something to hide.

She picked up her coffee-mug, wrapping her hands round it, gulping the fragrant liquid.

'But physically you still want him, is that it?'

She almost dropped the mug of coffee, the sudden involuntary movement of her body betraying her agitation.

'No, of course I——' She stopped, shaking her head, and told him huskily, 'John, please, this isn't something I want to discuss with you—with anyone.'

'It's all right,' he told her soothingly. 'I'm not trying to pry and I'm certainly not sitting in judgement. It is quite a common phenomenon, you know, Holly. One of the heaviest burdens our society has imposed on women is that of believing that love is synonymous with desire.

'I suppose he was your first lover...'

She stood up, thoroughly agitated. 'John, please...'

'I'm sorry. I'm your friend, Holly, I care about you. I want to help you, not hurt you. Who knows, maybe the best thing you could do would be to go to bed with him? You might just find that the reality is by no means as attractive as your memories.' He had finished his coffee and now he stood up. 'Of course, that's a man's view, a man's solution; women think and feel differently, but perhaps the only way for you to be free of him is for you to confront your physical desire for him instead of running away from it. One thing is certain; until you do, you'll never be free to admit another man into your life.'

Holly was still sitting down, her head bowed, her face averted from him, but he hadn't finished.

'I'm sorry if I've spoken out of turn, or hurt you in any way, but I hate seeing you like this. Tonight, half the time you weren't even with the rest of us. For your own sake you must find a way of either overcoming or accepting how you feel about him.'

He was heading for the door. Automatically Holly got up to go with him. At the front door, John paused and then turned towards her, kissing her briefly on the cheek. If he felt her instinctive recoil, he didn't show it, simply smiling wryly at her before saying quietly, 'It's all right, Holly, I know. Even without him, you wouldn't want me. At least not as a lover, but I hope that we're good enough friends for you to understand how concerned I am about you. Think about what I've said, won't you?'

Once he had gone, Holly went back to the kitchen and made herself a fresh mug of coffee.

She felt cold and sick inside, as shaky as though she had just suffered a trauma. She closed her eyes, biting on the inside of her bottom lip. If *John* had recognised how vulnerable she was to Robert, if he had guessed how much the past still haunted her, then how many other people, how many other friends were surreptitiously watching her...waiting...assessing?

She was becoming paranoid, she told herself. John had made a perceptive guess at how she felt and she had been foolish enough to confirm his suspicions, that was all.

But what she had said to John was true; she *didn't* love Robert. How could she? How could any woman love a man she couldn't trust—a man who had lied to her, who had deceived her, who had hurt her the way Robert had hurt her?

And as for this raw ache of physical need that tormented her so much... She swallowed past the tense muscles of her throat, feeling the pain of their rigid ache.

Perhaps John was right; perhaps the only way for her to overcome that torment was to—to what? Make love with Robert...to have sex with him?

The sensations churning her stomach made her tense her muscles in quick defensiveness. How could she do that? It was impossible. She would be far too afraid of losing control, of being once again the helpless girl who had been unable to stop herself from wanting him so intensely. She could remember even now how when he had held her, when he had kissed her, it had been like walking mindlessly into the deepest water, like feeling it close over her head and knowing she was drowning, helpless, and totally out of control. She couldn't put herself through that kind of torment again, that kind of humiliation; she couldn't allow herself to take that kind of risk.

But what if somehow or other she could maintain her self-control? What if she could prove both to herself and to Robert that he no longer had the power to touch her, to arouse her, to make her ache for him and want him to the point where nothing else mattered, where sanity and reality were unwanted barriers between them that she shed along with her clothes? If she could do that...if she could do that, wouldn't she, as John had suggested, finally be free?

She sipped her coffee shakily, telling herself that it must be the effect of the red wine that was making her think such dangerous and challenging thoughts.

'There's still this,' Robert had told her, and then he had kissed her, knowing that she would respond, knowing that she...

Shivering with nervous tension, she finished her coffee. It was gone one o'clock and she wanted to be up early in the morning. Mechanically she washed up and then went upstairs. Damn John for making her confront issues she would much rather have left undisturbed.

Following her date with John, Holly had one of the busiest weeks she could remember. There never seemed to be a minute for her to draw breath, never mind anything else, and yet in the evening every time the phone rang she found her stomach muscles tensing until she had answered the call and assured herself that it wasn't Robert on the other end of the line. There was no reason why he *should* ring her, she told herself, and yet at night she dreamed of him... dreamed that he was pursuing her while she fled through a growing tangle of undergrowth that quickly became darker and thicker, until what she actually wanted to do was not to run from him but to turn to him.

'You're losing weight,' Alice remarked, studying her. 'You don't eat enough.'

'Correction, I don't have enough *time* to eat,' Holly told her ruefully. 'The sooner Paul gets back, the better...'

'Mm... he won't be able to delay much longer, will he? There's the perfume launch...'

'Don't remind me,' Holly groaned. She had had a phone call from Elaine to discuss the media interviews she had organised for her, and the PR executive was still trying to coax her up to London for an image-polishing session.

'Why don't you go?' Alice urged her. 'Just think, a wardrobe full of new clothes and the chance to visit a top hair and make-up stylist.'

'Ten years ago I might have been tempted,' Holly told her. 'But now the thought of a lot of high-fashion stuff hanging unworn in my wardrobe seems such a waste...especially when I know that I'm going to spend most of my free time over the autumn and winter working in the garden in an old sweater of Paul's, a pair of jeans and my wellingtons.'

Alice laughed and then told her, 'I saw the most fabulous velour catsuits featured in a fashion mag the other day. Think of the effect you'd create on the local social scene, wearing one of them, and with your figure you could——'

'Don't,' Holly begged her. 'I'd probably be dropped from every guest list for fifty miles around...' She paused and then added with a grin, 'Perhaps I should try it.'

They both laughed and then Alice shook her head and warned her, 'You wait until Paul gets back. He'll back up Elaine and between the two of them——'

'Between the two of them they are not getting me into any velour catsuit,' Holly told her firmly.

'Shorts, then,' Alice teased her. 'They're very big this season as well.'

'Not on me, they're not going to be,' Holly assured her, then asked, 'Have you seen that estimate for those recyclable containers?'

Another week passed; she saw Robert only once, walking down the street towards her when she had been doing her shopping. He saw her and raised his hand, hurrying up to her with a smile.

Panic made her turn the other way and cross the street, pretending she hadn't seen or heard him.

Afterwards she was furious with herself for behaving so stupidly. When she got home the phone was ringing. She picked up the receiver and heard Robert saying her name.

Without saying a word, she slammed down the receiver and then stood ignoring its persistent ring. *Why* was he doing this to her? Surely no sane man would go to such lengths simply to reactivate an old love-affair—if that was what he wanted. His behaviour seemed so illogical.

Summer was virtually over. She had wanted to spend the weekend in the garden, but she had too much work to do. Instead, she spent it inside, at her desk, forgoing lunch and then supper as she tried to catch up with the backlog of work.

At eight o'clock when the phone rang, Holly stared at it with a frown, as though unsure of why it was ringing. She hesitated before reaching for the receiver, tensing as she half expected to hear Robert's voice on the other end of the line.

Instead, to her surprise, the voice she heard belonged to Paul.

'Hi. Guess where I am,' he demanded.

'I've no idea. Where are you?'

'Here, at home. Look, come round and bring a bottle of champagne with you. You and I have got something to celebrate.'

'You're *home*? But——'

'Come round,' Paul interrupted her. 'I'll tell you everything then.'

It was typical of her brother to arrive home early without any warning and then demand her presence, but for once Holly was too glad to have him back to object.

Paul had a small but very luxurious apartment several miles away in a large Victorian house which had been converted into a complex of apartments, with all the owners having access to a communal conservatory, the gardens, and a sports complex which included an indoor swimming-pool.

Having stopped on the way to buy a bottle of champagne, Holly waited for the automatic gates surrounding the property to open and admit her car, and then drove carefully up the drive to park in one of the spaces reserved for non-residents.

The apartments were guarded by a very sophisticated security system. She had to wait in the Gothic panelled hallway for Paul to authorise her entry, using the discreetly concealed lift to take her up to his apartment on the top floor.

The first thing she noticed when he opened the door was his tan; unlike her, he had not inherited their mother's fair skin, and his stay in South America had not only bleached his hair, but darkened his skin to mahogany. The second thing she noticed, just as she had finished telling him with sisterly candour that he looked like an advert for an American beach-boy, was that he wasn't alone.

Robert was standing in front of the sitting-room window, staring out into the night.

'Great, you've got the champagne,' Paul announced, ignoring her sarcastic comment. Shock hit her, paralysing her. What was Robert doing here?

'I met Robert at the airport. He was just seeing Angela off and he very kindly offered me a lift back. I've got some terrific news, Holly.'

'Why didn't you tell me you were coming home? I would have picked you up,' Holly asked him automatically.

'There wasn't time. When I heard I'd got the licences through, I went out to the airport to book a seat home and found that I could have a cancellation on a flight leaving within a couple of hours. There wasn't time for me to do anything more than rush back to my hotel, pack my stuff and get myself back to the airport.

'I've invited Robert to have supper with us. No point in going back to eat alone...'

'Supper? But...'

'Don't panic. I've ordered it from the restaurant.'

In addition to its other facilities, the complex also had a small restaurant for the use of residents and their guests, and although room service was not really provided Paul had somehow or other managed to charm his way around the catering staff.

'You haven't gone vegetarian, have you?' he asked her now, grinning at her.

It was a sore point between them. Holly very rarely ate meat of any kind, but she did enjoy fish, even while her conscience urged her to try seriously to convert to a wholly vegetarian diet.

'I just hope you haven't ordered me steak,' she told him.

She was still trying to get over the shock of Robert's presence. Had she known that he was going to be here, no way would she have come over.

'They'll be half an hour or so yet with supper, so let's open that champagne, shall we? Here you are, Rob, you do it. I'll get the glasses.'

Paul had disappeared in the direction of the kitchen, leaving Holly alone with Robert. She kept as much distance as she could between them, stiffening as she heard him saying quietly, 'This wasn't my idea, Holly, but that doesn't matter——' he stopped speaking as Paul walked back into the room.

The champagne was poured, and Paul handed Holly her glass.

'A toast,' he declared. 'To the rain forest and the iugyar plant.'

'The...' Holly paused, her glass halfway to her lips. '... the iugyar plant? What on earth's that?'

'It's a plant that grows in the rain forest. The native tribespeople use it on their skins. It heals sores and bites, and it also seems to have a rejuvenating effect on damaged skin. They make a kind of paste from the stems and leaves which they apply to the skin. I tried it myself. It certainly seems to work. Just think, Holly,' he carried on, excitement sharpening his voice, 'a natural plant remedy that actually slows down the ageing process.'

'You said it healed bites and wounds,' Holly reminded him dubiously.

'So it does, but I also said that it heals them remarkably quickly. If the majority of the ageing process is caused by sun damage, then might not it heal that equally effectively? It obviously possesses something that makes the skin repair itself far faster than normal...something that accelerates the healing and thus the growth process of the skin.

'Of course we won't know how effective it might be until we've researched it properly.'

'And done clinical tests,' Holly reminded him. 'Tests which must not be carried out on animals.'

'I know. I know,' Paul soothed. 'But think of the potential if it can be proved that it actually does slow down the ageing process. Oh, come on, show a little bit more enthusiasm,' he begged her.

'I...I don't know what to say,' Holly admitted. 'On the face of it it sounds a wonderful discovery...'

'She's always like this,' Paul complained wryly to Robert. 'Show Holly a glimpse of paradise, and she'd be saying that it was only a mirage. I've never known such a doubting Thomas. You never used to be like this,' he told her.

'I've got the business to think of,' Holly told him unsteadily. 'We can't afford to take chances. We don't know anything about this plant as yet...about what adverse effects it may have.'

'Oh, Holly. You're always looking for problems...always so dubious and distrustful,' Paul told her. 'Always so cautious.'

'One of us has to be,' Holly pointed out, and then added, 'I'm sorry, Paul. Of course I'm thrilled and excited, but...'

'But what?'

'Well, nothing. It's just that it seems almost too good to be true,' she told him helplessly.

A knock on the door interrupted them. Paul went to answer it and came back pushing a covered dinner-wagon.

'Supper is served,' he announced, 'and out of respect to you, Holly, my love, none of us is eating steak. In fact Robert seems to share your squeamishness—he opted for fish as well. I've ordered salmon for you, by the way. Hope that's OK?'

'Lovely,' Holly assured him.

'Well, finish your champagne, then,' Paul instructed her. 'I've opened wine to have with our meal.'

Obediently Holly gulped down the fizzing liquid, gasping a little at the shock of the cold bubbles against the back of her throat and inside her stomach.

As she headed for Paul's small dining-room, she recognised that she felt distinctly unsteady on her feet.

Robert obviously thought so as well, because as she reached the door he moved unobtrusively to her side, touching her arm lightly as though gently supporting her.

Paul was too busy pouring the wine to see what was going on. A fine tremor of sensation ran through Holly's body, as her senses reacted to Robert's proximity. She wanted to move away from him, to snap at him to take his arm away, but at the same time she was agonisingly conscious of an equally strong and completely conflicting desire to

let go of the past and with it all her antagonism
and to simply stand there, secure in the knowledge
that it was unnecessary for her to say or do anything; that he would instinctively know her needs,
her fears, her——

She shivered suddenly, causing Paul, who had
turned round, to frown and exclaim, 'You're cold!
I'll put the heating on. Come and sit down.'

Shakily she did so, wanting to sit as far away
from Robert as she could and yet somehow dis-
covering that she was actually sitting between the
two men.

As old friends, it was natural that they had a lot
of catching up to do and yet Robert made a point
of making sure that she was included in the
conversation.

In any other circumstances, had she been meeting
him for the first time, she knew that she would have
found him not just a physically compelling and very
attractive man, but that she would also have been
impressed both by his intellect and his respect for
hers.

He hadn't always been like that. As a younger
man he had been inclined, like Paul, to overrule
her judgements, to take a lordly, masculine and
very, very annoying attitude towards any attempt
on her part to claim equal intelligence and
awareness of current situations.

Now, without any of the obsequious fawning that
made her feel so uncomfortable and which she
always felt was both false and hypocritical, he made
it plain that he was genuinely interested in her opinions, her comments.

It was Paul who asked him why he had come back, and if he intended to run his business from the Hall.

'Yes, in answer to your second question,' he responded promptly and then hesitated before adding, 'As for your first...well, let's just say that I'd always had in mind to come back and that suddenly I felt that I didn't want to delay returning any longer.'

'Mm...well, it's going to be quite a change, giving up New York to live here.'

'A welcome one, I can assure you,' Robert told him quietly.

'So you've no more ambitions...no more mountains to climb?' Paul asked.

Robert shook his head.

'I do have ambitions...or at least one very important one. I hear you're launching a new perfume range this autumn,' he commented, turning to Holly.

'Yes, we are.'

'The launch is a bit of a sore point so far as Holly is concerned,' Paul told him. 'She's very anti any kind of media attention, but, as I've told her, to succeed in the market place these days you have to bring your product to the attention of that market——'

'Maybe so, but I object to having to be forced into an over-glamourised and totally false image that can be held up to the general public as the way a successful businesswoman of the nineties should look,' Holly interrupted him.

'It's what people expect. It's a very well-known fact that people like to look up to others, to be a little in awe of them,' said Robert.

'Tell her, Robert. In fact, I think that perhaps you and I ought to get together, you know. We could do with some good management consultancy. We're expanding so rapidly now——'

'Perhaps we're expanding too rapidly,' Holly interjected, but Paul had stopped listening to her and was enthusiastically outlining to Robert his dreams of taking the company on to international fame.

'I'm not sure that's a good idea,' Robert told him. 'There's a very definite move away from over-expansion. Too many companies that were highly successful in their own field have found themselves in deep financial difficulties because of over-expansion. These days people who are market leaders are beginning to recognise that staying small can sometimes be best, especially with a concern like yours, when you are very, very reliant on your reputation and good name.'

While they argued, Holly sipped her wine. She had not been able to eat all her salmon, even though she had been hungry. The taut muscles of her stomach had made it impossible for her to relax, perhaps if she drank her wine that might help.

She smothered a yawn and then another, and then finally, knowing that if she didn't make a move soon she was all too likely to fall asleep where she was, she turned to Paul and apologised.

'I'm going to have to go, Paul. I'm sorry, but I'm rather tired.'

'OK, I'll go and ring for a taxi for you.'

'A taxi? But I've got my car.'

'And you've also had a full glass of champagne and three glasses of wine,' Paul told her. 'You can't drive, Holly, even if you could manage to stay awake at the wheel, it wouldn't be safe.'

'No... I suppose you're right,' she acknowledged reluctantly.

'There's no need for Holly to get a taxi,' she heard Robert saying. 'I've got my car here and I have to go past the farm on my way home. I could drop her off.'

'Oh, no. I couldn't put you to that trouble,' Holly protested, shocked out of her lethargic state as she suddenly realised her danger.

'It's no trouble,' Robert assured her. 'And besides, at this time on a Saturday evening you could have quite a long wait for a cab.'

'Robert's right,' Paul agreed, grinning a little as he looked at her heavy eyes. 'You'll have to watch her, Rob. She'll probably fall asleep on you. What have you been doing, Holly? Too many heavy dates, I suppose,' he teased her.

'No, too many hours spent at my desk trying to keep on top of the paperwork,' Holly corrected him.

'Sorry, sis,' Paul apologised, leaning forward to ruffle her hair and kiss her. 'That's my fault, I know, but things should get a lot easier now that I'm back.'

As they all stood up and walked towards the hall he shook hands with Robert and said genially, 'Thanks for the lift home, Rob, and we'll have to get together some time soon.'

Already it was too late for her to protest that she would prefer to make her own way home, Holly recognised as Paul unlocked the door for them and Robert waited politely for her to precede him through it.

In the lift they stood together in silence, neither of them looking at the other. She didn't want this, Holly recognised nervously. She didn't want to be on her own with Robert . . . didn't want the vulnerability, the awareness, the re-awakening of everything that she had fought so hard to put behind her.

CHAPTER EIGHT

SOMEWHERE between Paul's flat and her own home, Holly fell instantly and deeply asleep, and, while she wasn't aware of the problems this was likely to cause, Robert most certainly was.

He glanced at her once briefly, thinking that her averted profile and her silence were merely a further indication of her unwillingness to have anything to do with him, a well-deserved reminder that he had long ago lost any rights he might have had to her friendship...or her love, and then some sixth sense alerted him to the fact that she had simply fallen asleep.

He slowed down so that he could check, exhaling slowly, like someone trying to control the betraying rapidity of his accelerated breathing, as he looked into her sleeping face.

If anything, she was more desirable now, more womanly, more...more everything than she had been as a girl, or was it simply that he, as a man and not a boy, was just more aware of all that she was, all that she would have to give to the man lucky enough to be loved by her?

Once he could have been that man, but he had turned his back on her, had told himself that he was too young, that they were both too young—that they would forget one another and get on with their lives. He had had such plans...plans he had made long before that summer when he had looked at Paul's kid sister and felt his body tighten with desire and his heart with emotion.

His father had suffered ill health all his life and had retired early on a very meagre pension, and his mother had constantly warned Robert of the fate that would befall him if he ever fell into the same trap as his father. He had loved his father with an almost parental protectiveness, aching sometimes for the look of helpless defeat he could see in his eyes and yet at the same time he had sworn that he would never be like him.

Both his parents were now dead, and as an adult he fully recognised that his father might have been quite content with his garden, his friends, his quiet life, if his mother had also been able to accept it; he had also come to learn that wealth, ambition, success did not necessarily make a man happy, that there were other things in life, other needs, other appetites which, if starved, could turn worldly success into an arid desert where a man could die of thirst.

He had known almost from the time he left her that he would never truly be able to forget Holly, and after less than six months away from her he had ached so intensely for her that he had often woken up in the night with his face wet with tears and the echoes of her name still resounding through his mind as he called despairingly for her.

But then he had been too young, too selfish, too obsessed by the lessons he had absorbed from his parents' marriage to be prepared to admit that he had made a mistake, and then, by the time he was ready to admit it, it had been too late. He had told himself that Holly would have found someone else, that some other man with more sense and more wisdom than him would have seen all that he had deliberately refused to see.

For that reason he had not kept in touch with anyone from the village, and then he had started reading small items in the British financial Press about Holly's success. He had made the decision to move back to Britain. He had told himself that he was acting like a fool... that he was chasing a dream which was long dead... that he could well find out that the Holly he remembered no longer existed.

And then he had seen her, spoken to her and he had known immediately that nothing had changed—not for him, anyway, and all the emotions he had dammed up for so long had swamped him. That first time he had seen her on the lane the temptation then to take hold of her and to go on holding her had been so strong, he had had to physically restrain himself from reaching out to her.

He loved her, but did she, *could* she love him? Physically she was aware of him, desired him—he knew that. But was that desire merely an ancient long shadow cast by the past, or was it something he could build on, fan into real life... into real love? As he studied her sleeping face, he ached inside to stop the car and take hold of her, to whisper her name against her mouth, to tell her how much he loved her, how much he wanted her, so much that already his body—— He cursed under his breath, reminding himself that he was closer now to forty than to twenty and that the turbulent, uncontrollable reaction of his body to the merest thought of touching her was the reaction of an immature boy, not an adult man.

When they reached the farm Holly was still asleep. Her handbag was on the floor at her feet, and, acting on an impulse which he knew to be dangerous, he picked it up, hesitating before opening it. If he couldn't see her keys immediately, then he would wake her up. If he... But as soon as he opened her bag, he could see the dull gleam of a bunch of keys.

A sense of fatefulness pulsed through him, an absurd feeling that he wasn't acting wholly under his own control any more. A cop-out, he derided himself, as he removed the keys and closed Holly's handbag.

When he got out of the car and walked up the path to her front door, he could hear the frantic pulse of his own blood as it surged through his veins, dangerously laced with the adrenalin of excitement and danger.

He unlocked the front door, refusing to allow himself to dwell on what was running through his mind, on the thoughts that lay beneath the surface, like so many jagged rocks just below the waterline. Outwardly he was all calm control, his physical movements controlled and easy; inwardly... inwardly... Robert gave a small shudder, refusing to allow himself time to think, to reason. There was after all still time for Holly to wake up—still time for her to look at him with those huge eyes, which had once glowed with love...with adoration almost for him, but which now studied him with cool disdain, with contempt sometimes. That was a hard thing for a man to bear, especially when he...

When he what? When he had realised far, far too late that he loved her and he always would love her.

He opened the passenger door of the car, holding his breath as the light came on, but Holly didn't even move. He bent down, sliding one arm beneath her knees and the other around her back, as he eased her out of the car.

She weighed even less than he had expected. He remembered how fragile she had always felt; how small and feminine. Now her body was more mature, her waist narrower, her breasts and her hips rounder, her legs more slender.

Where she had been a girl, now she was a woman, and as he stood in the dark outside his car, holding her in his arms, he was excruciatingly aware of that fact.

The clouds which had previously obscured it rolled away from the face of the moon so that unexpectedly Holly's face was bathed in its light.

Robert held his breath as she tensed and frowned, half of him wanting her to wake up, to stop what was happening now before events went totally out of his control; the other half...

She made a small sound, her lips parting. Her hand moved, clutching at the front of his shirt, her frown deepened, her eyelashes quivering as though she were about to open her eyes, and then unbelievably she turned her face into his body. He heard the soft, pleased sound she made as her breath touched his skin. The physical reaction that stormed through him brought him out in a rash of goose-bumps and made him tremble.

Once, long ago, a lifetime ago, he could re-member her shyly kissing his throat, caressing his skin with lips so hesitant and tentative that his ache of need had made him grit his teeth and will himself not to take hold of her and...

Now that need was just as intense, but now he was less selfish, more aware, more concerned with the pleasure he wanted to give her than the pleasure he wanted for himself. Now his pleasure would be not so much in feeling her touch his skin, his flesh, but in being able to touch hers, in knowing that she welcomed his touch—that she wanted it...that she wanted *him*...and that she welcomed that wanting.

He could feel the painful burn of the emotion that choked his throat and stung his eyes. Holly, Holly; he fought back a mad impulse to wake her up and tell her how much he loved her, how much he had missed her.

Shuddering a little, he turned round and walked towards the front door.

The farmhouse felt warm and welcoming. The square hallway was flagged, its stones worn and polished. A heavy damask curtain covered the back of the front door, its fabric rich and worn. A pol-ished table held a pewter jug of garden flowers. Pewter wall-lights illuminated the plastered walls. Several doors opened off the hallway, but Robert's glance was drawn upwards to the stairs, their wooden treads, like the stone floor, were worn and polished, a strip of carpet fastened by old-fashioned stair-rods covered their centre, its faded reds, creams and blues soft and easy on the eye.

He started up the stairs, his arms tensing now under Holly's weight.

He was only doing the sensible thing, he assured himself. Better for her to wake up lying comfortably on top of her bed than cramped upright in a chair.

Only one of the bedroom doors was open. He took a chance and carried her into that room.

There was a neat pile of clean laundry on the wooden chest at the bottom of the bed, and a towelling robe had been discarded on the bed, its whiteness a sharp blur of light on the muted colours of the patchwork quilt.

Instinct made him pull back the quilt before depositing Holly on the bed. It was old and, he suspected, valuable. As he released her from the captivity of his arms, Holly frowned and then moved seekingly on the bed, her frown deepening. She shivered as though suddenly cold.

The bedroom window was open. Robert moved across to close it and with it the curtains. The room was decorated in soft shades of peach, grey and blue, the furniture was old and well polished, a huge salt-glazed jug of bleached-out dried seed-heads and flowers stood on one of the chests.

On the table beside the bed was a heavy, very battered and ancient-looking book. Robert picked it up, a deep, smiling curve indenting his mouth as he read the title. *Culpeper's Complete Herbal*.

Of course... what else? Holly was still asleep. By rights he ought to go and leave her in peace.

His responsibility, his duty to her was now finished. There was nothing to keep him here. No reason for him to stay. And yet somehow he couldn't leave. He walked towards the door, and then hesitated, before walking back again to stand looking down at her. He reached out and touched her face, tracing the fragile bone-structure, smoothing his fingertip along her eyebrows.

His hand trembled; he should not be doing this. It was an intrusion of the worst kind... a voyeurism... a theft of her privacy. He repeated to himself all the reasons why he should leave, but none of them made any sense, not when he wanted to be with her so much, not when this room, with its ancient warmth, its awareness of the frailties of human nature, its silent holding of the secrets of all the lovers who had shared its privacy and solitude, seemed to murmur to him that there was no reason for him to go and every reason for him to stay, that his place was here with this woman, and that it always had been and always would be.

He removed his shoes and jacket. All he wanted to do was to lie beside her, to deceive himself if only for a little while that it *was* possible to go back... that it was possible for her to forget, to forgive... that his love would be enough to reactivate hers.

He lay down on the bed beside her, facing her, but not touching her.

For a long time he simply watched her, letting his senses absorb the reality of her. He yawned once, twice, a third time, his eyes closing.

The last thing he did before he fell asleep was to reach out and curl his arm protectively and possessively around her waist.

Holly woke up first, deliciously aware of a feeling of warmth and pleasure, a sensation of being held, protected . . . of being loved almost.

She lay where she was, happily absorbing the sensation that filled her body with such pleasure and her mind with such happiness, letting herself relax, letting herself move closer to that wonderful source of warmth and comfort, that male body that lay so tantalisingly close to her own.

Abruptly she opened her eyes. No, her brain *wasn't* playing tricks on her. She *was* actually lying against the bulk of another body—of Robert's body, she recognised on a sudden body-stiffening surge of shocked awareness.

For a moment she was totally confused, unable to understand what on earth she was doing lying on her bed with Robert, both of them apparently fully dressed, their bodies entwined like those of the closest and most passionate of lovers.

She started to tremble, too bemused to even think of moving away from him. At her side Robert woke up, his eyes opening just as she was studying him.

Her breath caught in her throat, a reactionary surge of sensation gripping her body.

'Holly.'

Her name on his lips sounded like the breath of life itself. Her own heartbeat ceased and then rocked dangerously against her chest wall.

She had moved, must have moved, because suddenly she was closer to him, much, much closer.

'Holly.'

He said her name again, breathing against her lips so that she trembled.

She already knew the taste of his mouth, its shape and its texture, just as she knew her own response to his kiss, and yet still she wasn't prepared for it...wasn't ready for the frighteningly intense kickback of emotion and need that burst through her, so that without even having to think about it she was clinging to him, wanting him, needing him, loving him, all the years apart dissolving in the heat that burned so strongly inside her.

Almost as though she were still asleep and wrapped in the protected delusion of a longed-for and familiar dream, Holly allowed herself to be carried by the floodtide of her emotions.

This was Robert who held her, who touched her, who kissed her. This was Robert's skin beneath her own trembling fingertips, Robert's mouth caressing her own with tenderness and hunger, Robert's voice that told her brokenly and achingly how much he wanted her, how much he had longed for this moment, how much he still ached for her.

Holly herself said nothing, too enraptured by the unbelievable wonder of what was happening to be able to speak.

Robert's lips caressed her throat, finding the familiarly vulnerable spot just where her neck ran into her shoulder, the pressure of his mouth hardening as he felt the shudder that tormented her body and heard her husky moan of pleasure.

As she twisted up against him, clinging to him, trembling with arousal and need, Holly was aware of the irritating barrier of their clothes, of her need to feel against her the satin hardness of his body, the slightly rough abrasion of his body hair, the familiar caress of his hands.

She made a husky, importunate sound beneath her breath, its message so subtle that if Robert hadn't recognised it he would not have known what it meant. His heart seemed to leap inside his chest, his hands trembling as he complied with her unspoken demand.

It had been a long time since he had done anything like this... since he had *wanted* to do anything like this, he admitted, hating the sour memory of the disastrous attempts he had made to drown out the memory of her body with someone else. After a while he had acknowledged that what he was doing was as damaging to himself as it was to his unfortunate partners and had accepted the unexpected celibacy of his life with a certain grim self-mockery.

Holly, of course, would not have been so chaste, but then why should she be? This was an age when her sex was unfettered by the unfair bondage once imposed on it by his, and, knowing there must have been other men had lessened neither his love for her, nor his respect, even though he was bitterly jealous and envious of the gifts she had given them. Gifts which once he himself had so easily and so immaturely spurned.

Now, though, he was here with her and he would show her just how much he had changed, just how much he appreciated all that she was... all that she had once given him.

As she finally managed to unfasten and push away her shirt, he promised himself that he would make for her such a feast of adoration and loving that his own desire would be totally unimportant to him and that all his pleasure would be in giving her, showing her just how much she meant to him, and then she moved and he saw through the fragile silk of her bra the dark areolae of her nipples and their taut, swollen thrust.

He moved, without knowing what he was doing, an uncoordinated, jerky movement that brought his hand briefly into contact with her body.

She breathed deeply and quickly, the movement pushing her breasts against the fine silk, so that it seemed as though her flesh was silently begging for his touch.

As he bent his head, Holly felt the heat of his breath against her breast-bone. She tensed, looking down on the dark thickness of his hair. She could feel the heat coming off his skin, sense his tension and his arousal.

When his mouth touched the satin slope of her breast, she shuddered a little, unable to move, unable to breathe, unable to do anything other than close her eyes and whisper his name as if it were a litany of prayer for fulfilment as she felt his mouth moving hungrily against her skin, pushing at the silky barrier that kept him from his goal, and then, as though he was too impatient or too aroused to be able to remove it, sliding over it, taking the fabric into his mouth along with the hard peak of her breast.

Once, long ago, he had caressed her like this and then as now she had cried out as the tiny needle-sharp darts of sensation pierced her body and convulsed her womb. Then Holly had been half afraid, half shocked by the intensity of what she was experiencing. Now...

She gave a long shudder of delicious pleasure, arching her back, sliding her hands over Robert's shoulder and into his nape, holding him against her body as she gasped his name and felt his own body shudder in response to what was happening to her.

After that everything was like a dream, time flowing like an ever-increasing river, carrying her with it, so that there was only the touch of his hands, the sound of their breathing and always, always the endless unbearable pleasure stretching her on a rack of exquisite sensation so that she turned and twisted against him, calling out his name, sometimes in a plea, sometimes in an unmeant denial.

Beneath her hands his back felt hard and smooth. She felt his muscles compress beneath the involuntary tightening drag of her nails.

He kissed her belly and then her thighs, the deliberately tender touch of his mouth slowing down time so that every tiny degree of each second seemed to hang in space, every touch holding a lifetime of sensation and desire.

Once, as a girl, she had trembled on the brink of the intimacy they were sharing now, and had withdrawn from it, afraid both of it and of her own response to it. Although she hesitated, it was the merest hesitation, and was soon swept away, over-

whelmed by her body's instinctive awareness of all
that such intimacy meant, her senses drowning
under the slow lap of his tongue, her body turning
fluid and weightless, wanting, needing him with so
much intensity that that wanting became a confused string of husky words punctuated by the fe-
vered tension of her writhing body. Her release
when it came was almost too intense to be borne,
so sharply pleasurable that it made her cry out to
him...*for* him, knowing with some deeply atav-
istic instinct that she wanted him almost more than
she had wanted that selflessly given release.

For a moment Robert hesitated. She heard him
mutter something—a protest, a question, her bemused senses could not define the words, only his
hesitation.

She touched his body and felt him tremble.

'I want you, Robert. I want *you*,' she told him,
and as she said the words they became the truth,
her body sleek and unexpectedly seductive, as she
touched him, held him and almost wantonly incited
him to abandon his self-control and move against
her and then at last within her.

The unexpected sensation of tightness, of
newness shocked them both, causing a stillness, a
tension between them.

'Holly...'

Robert was looking at her, studying her. She
wanted to close her eyes, to evade that seeking,
almost puzzled scrutiny.

'You feel so small...so—so much like the first
time...'

The words were too probing, too painful, bringing back into sharp focus the reality of what was happening, and reality was the last thing Holly wanted right now. Facing reality meant admitting to herself just what she was doing and why. Facing reality meant...

'I...I don't want to hurt you.'

He had said that the first time, she remembered achingly, and even though she had wanted him she had still been a little afraid. But he hadn't hurt her—far from it—and he wouldn't hurt her now either.

She let her body relax, and moved against him, feeling the shudder of arousal he couldn't control, and suddenly welcoming it, welcoming him, abandoning herself to the sensation of her body moving softly and sweetly to embrace his.

Less had changed than he had thought, his love for her making a mockery of his maturity and imagined self-control, Robert acknowledged shakily as he was caught up in the maelstrom of his own desire.

Knowing he was no longer in control, he called out to her, his voice raw with anguish and pain. He thought he heard her own voice speak back in response, its timbre soft with love, but he was far too caught up in his own climax to do much more than distantly register it with tormented wonder, as he tried to tell her how much he had wanted there to be more time, more pleasure, more control so that he could have shown her, told her, convinced her of how much he had always loved her and always would.

CHAPTER NINE

'HOLLY.'

Crossly Holly rolled over, trying to ignore the lure of the male voice speaking her name. She didn't want to wake up; something nagged at the corner of her mind, some reason . . . some unpleasantness, some *thing* that was warning her that it would be better to stay asleep, but the voice was repeating her name. She could feel a warm breath brushing her skin, a hand gently shaking her shoulder.

Sighing, she opened her eyes and then froze, shock, disbelief, and then finally the haunting agony of awareness and remembrance rolling over her.

'It's gone nine and I really ought to leave, but I wanted to speak to you first . . . to . . .'

She could hear the hesitation, the reluctance—the regret?—in Robert's voice and sickeningly she became aware of everything that had happened during the night. Even without moving, she was explicitly and intensely aware of the difference within her own body, the betrayal it had caused her to suffer.

Again that hesitation, that reluctance . . . that sense of knowing that he was hunting for the right words—for the right excuse, she reflected bitterly. But what possible excuse was there? None—at least not for her. For him it was different, he was a man, and as such...

She could feel the heavy, aching press of tears at the back of her eyes and throat, the beginnings of a frantic panic, which, if she wasn't careful, would get totally out of control. Feverishly she tried to remember just what she had done... just what she had said...just how much she might have betrayed.

That they had made love, passionately, intensely, sensually, she could not deny; it was a knowledge from which she had no means of escape. All she could do now was to salvage what could be salvaged...to remind herself of just why Robert was standing looking at her with such remorse, such unease. It had been her fault and not his if she had recklessly and wantonly squandered on him the gift of the love he did not want...her fault if—if what? They had been lovers? Was that entirely *her* fault? She shivered, knowing that she could not remember, that she could only remember the sharp sweetness of waking up and finding him beside her, of that first moment when he had touched her, kissed her, after that... After that her only memories had nothing to do with reality and everything to do with such intangibles as feelings, emotions, needs and desires.

'Holly...'

She turned away from him, making her voice sound as crisp as she could as she lied self-protectingly, 'There's no need for you to say anything, Robert. Last night was something that was probably bound to happen—a catharsis, perhaps,

for both of us ... a final, if somewhat drastic way
of finally drawing a line under the past.

'Not long ago you accused me of wanting you.
You were right ... I *did* want you. But now ...' She
took a deep breath and curled her fingers into her
palms so that her nails bit into the tender flesh and
she lied desperately, 'But now I don't want you any
more. You see, I realised last night that I was simply
clinging on to an idea—a foolish, teenage dream
that bore no resemblance at all to reality. I don't
regret what happened. It's finally freed me from
the past ... finally enabled me to do what I should
have done years ago ... finally freed me to find—
to find someone else. So you see there's no need
for you to say anything, or to worry that I might
misunderstand what happened. I'm a woman
now...an adult. Last night was something that had
to happen. But now that it has ...' She took a deep
breath. 'Now that it has, I think we'd both agree
that it would be best if from now on we both went
our separate ways.'

'If that's what you want.'

His voice was unexpectedly toneless and flat for
a man who had just had the good fortune to be
freed from all responsibility and guilt for his ac-
tions, Holly thought bitterly, but she didn't turn
round to look at him and so didn't recognise his
shock nor see the sudden savage shimmer of tears
that moistened his eyes before he blinked them
away.

'That's exactly what I want,' she told him fiercely,
keeping her voice tight in case he heard the emotion

she was trying to control; in case he guessed the truth.

She heard him walk towards the door, heard it open . . . heard his feet on the stairs and then the front door opening and closing. As she lay there, tense and hesitant, she heard him start up his car.

She waited until she was sure he had driven away, until the last notes of the car engine had faded, before giving way to her emotions, and then she rolled over on to her stomach and lay there, dry-eyed, wanting to cry, aching for the release of tears and yet knowing that her pain went too deep for that release.

How had she ever managed to delude herself that she no longer loved him? And how could *he* be so blind? Surely a fool could have read the signs, could have, would have known that no woman could ever respond to a man the way she had responded to him last night if she had not loved him so over-whelmingly, so totally that nothing else mattered.

She told herself savagely that she ought to be pleased that he had not known, that she *ought* to have been pleased at this further evidence of his imperfections, of his flaws; but it made no difference. All she could cling to now was the relief of knowing that at least she had had the presence of mind, the pride to find a way of reclaiming her shattered self-respect by telling him that last night had simply been the means of drawing a line under the past, of separating herself from it.

And thank God that he *had* believed her; but then he had every reason to, hadn't he? She could well imagine the panic, the distaste, the dread that must have overwhelmed him when he woke up and found himself lying beside her, when he remembered... He must have been dreading her waking up and attempting to make some kind of emotional claim on him. Did he think she would have behaved as she had done as a girl; that she would cry and plead, that she would abandon her pride and her self-respect to beg him to tell her that he loved her, that he wanted her? Yes, he must have been relieved ... more than relieved by her reaction. And yet he had not shown it, had not indicated that he was aware of how difficult she might be finding the situation.

Her memories of last night were filled with the shimmering, taunting, haunting sense of having known great tenderness...of having been given such an outpouring of exquisite care that her mouth compressed as she taunted herself for her folly and self-deceit. What had happened between them had simply been sex, on his part at least. If *she* wanted to cloak that need in the flattering, dangerous robes of other non-existent emotions, then she would have to pay the price for that folly.

Why torment herself? Why inflict that kind of pain on herself? Why not simply admit the truth— that last night, motivated by physical desire, Robert had once again been her lover and that in the chilling light of the new day he had instantly regretted that weakness?

As she lay shivering, suddenly and repugnantly aware of how strongly the scent of both Robert and the night still clung to her skin and her bed, Holly clung gratefully to the knowledge that the intensity of the workload that lay ahead of her over the coming months was such that it would give her scant time to dwell on what had happened.

Work, the eternal panacea—if there *was* a panacea for this kind of pain, this kind of wanting . . . this kind of angry self-loathing . . . this kind of helpless, hopeless longing for a man who she knew did not share her feelings.

Somehow she managed to drag herself through the rest of the week, although not without both Alice and Paul asking her anxiously what was wrong.

'I'm just a bit run-down,' she told them both, not entirely untruthfully.

She found that she was almost totally unable to eat, and dogged by a desire to simply curl up and go to sleep and let the rest of the world go on without her.

She didn't need anyone to tell her what she was suffering from; unrequited love was an almost risible malady in these modern times, and as she dragged herself miserably through yet another day she wondered how many of her fellow human beings were right at this moment suffering from the same despair, from something which was almost a taboo in these high-achieving, having-it-all nineties. That morning she had read a piece about the company in a magazine. The article had focused more on her than on the company, putting her forward as a thoroughly modern woman—a woman who had everything in her life that she wanted.

Everything she wanted... She had nothing, nothing at all... not even the hope of having conceived Robert's child. Until this morning she hadn't known how much she had wanted to have that child. She shuddered a little, knowing that desire must be the ultimate form of folly; knowing that she had no right to inflict on a child the burden of being the sole focus of her emotions, to transfer to it the love Robert did not want.

She ought to be glad that she had not conceived, but instead she had wept bitter, acid tears... the tears of corroding anguish and despair, the tears she had not cried that morning when Robert had finally walked away from her.

In an attempt to force herself to try and get her life back to normal she agreed to accompany Paul to a mutual friend's dinner party on Saturday evening.

They arrived a little late, Paul having been delayed in picking her up by a telephone call, but their hostess, who had always had a soft spot for Holly's brother, smilingly forgave them as Paul expressed his apologies and produced the flowers he had bought for her.

'Go straight through to the drawing-room,' Gemma instructed them. 'Alan will get you both a drink, while I go and check on dinner. Everyone else has already arrived.

The Baileys lived in an elegant Georgian house which had been painstakingly renovated and decorated; their drawing-room was a large, beautifully proportioned room, decorated in warm shades of muted apricot and gold—a little theatrical perhaps for Holly's taste, but very, very elegant, and a perfect setting for the dinner-suited men and the women in their expensive designer outfits.

The Baileys were more Paul's friends than hers, but Alan Bailey greeted them both equally warmly as he came over to welcome them.

Holly refused a drink, glancing round the room while Paul explained how he had been delayed. Her interest in her fellow guests was half-hearted and vague, but then suddenly she froze, her body going cold and then hot as it reacted to the shock of seeing Robert standing on the other side of the room.

Fortunately he had his back to her, thus giving her time to make some attempt to get herself under control without his witnessing her puerile behaviour.

'What is it, what's wrong?' Paul questioned her in concern as their host excused himself.

'It's nothing. I...I think I've got a cold coming on, that's all,' Holly lied wildly.

'A cold?' Paul's eyebrows rose. 'You looked as though you were about to pass out.' He frowned. 'You're losing weight as well, Holly. Look, I know you're not keen on all the publicity surrounding the launch of the new perfume range, and I know that while I've been away the responsibility for my side of things as well as your own has all been down to you. If it's all getting too much for you...'

Holly shook her head.

'I'm just a bit run-down, that's all,' she told him once again. And, after all, it wasn't a lie. No, her deceit was in allowing Paul to believe that the cause of her ill health lay with her work instead of with her emotions.

Robert still hadn't seen her and she longed desperately to be able to escape before he did, but how could she leave without dragging Paul away as well, without drawing people's attention to her? No, she would just have to grit her teeth and somehow or other manage to get through the evening.

She glanced round the room again, achingly trying not to focus on Robert and yet helpless to stop herself from focusing on him, from wondering whom he was with. Not Angela—there was no sign of her—and not all the other guests were familiar to her so that it was impossible to work out which of the elegantly dressed women was Robert's partner.

Gemma returned to announce that dinner was about to be served.

The crimson dining-room with its antique furniture and heavy gilt-edged landscapes was an ideal setting to show off the Sèvres dinner service and the antique silver which the Baileys had recently acquired.

As much as an investment as anything else, so Alan explained as several of the female guests admired the delicate intricacy of the service.

As they all took their places, Holly discovered to her horror that Robert was seated opposite her. He gave her one piercing glance before sitting down. She felt her face grow hot. Her hands were shaking so much, she had to conceal them beneath the table. On her left Paul was talking to the woman seated next to him, oblivious of her distress.

Robert wasn't, though. In that one brief second before she had looked wildly away she had seen his mouth compress as though in anger and contempt.

All right, so she was behaving stupidly, showing for anyone who cared to look her lack of self-control and emotional vulnerability, but it had never occurred to her that Robert would be here. If it had ... if it had, she would never have agreed to come. She was still far too emotionally unstable to handle seeing him in the flesh ... still too acutely aware of him in all the ways that a woman *was* aware of a man whom she loved and who had been her lover.

Just knowing he was there now released such a flood of sensation inside her that she felt physically sick with the strain of suppressing it.

She couldn't allow herself to look at him again, dared not do so, and yet as though she were some helpless creature unable to control her own reactions she found that she was lifting her head and looking across the table at him.

He was speaking to the woman seated next to him, an incredibly chic brunette with an American accent, who, Holly realised as she heard them talking, was Robert's partner for the evening.

Jealousy stabbed her with red-hot knives of agonising pain, emotions she had never expected to experience, emotions so primeval that they shocked and distressed her, tormenting her on a rack of frantic anguish.

Were they lovers, Robert and this chic New Yorker? Had Robert's pursuit of her simply been fuelled by his desire for this woman who was now

seated beside him, who from their conversation had
obviously flown over from New York expressly to
see him? Lovers, of course they were lovers. She
was a fool if she allowed herself to think anything
else.

Now it was more important than ever that she
saw the meal through, that she smiled and talked,
that she did not allow anyone—but most especially
Robert and his lover—to guess just what she was
feeling.

By the time they had reached their main course,
Holly's head felt as though it were about to burst.
Each mouthful of food threatened to choke her and
when Robert's woman companion leaned across the
table and smiled warmly at her, exclaiming, 'I've
heard so much about you! Can I say how much I
admire you and all that you've achieved?' Holly
could only respond with an attempt at a polite smile
and a disjointed response. Candice was so patently
confident of her position in Robert's life, her
manner was so frank and open, so charming and
warm that in any other circumstances Holly knew
she must have liked her and been drawn towards
her.

As it was, she was conscious of a sick despair in
the knowledge that she was even being denied the
panacea of disliking the woman that Robert had
chosen as his lover, mingled with guilt and self-
contempt at her own behaviour. If she had known
that there was another woman in Robert's life, a
woman who believed that she had the exclusive right
to his desire, she would never had allowed her own
emotions to get so dangerously out of control,

would never have allowed herself to make love with Robert.

Everyone else had finished their main course. Gemma frowned a little as she removed Holly's half-full plate.

'I'm sorry, Gemma,' Holly apologised huskily. 'It was lovely but I...I just don't seem to have much of an appetite these days.'

As she turned back to the table, she was suddenly aware that Robert was watching her intently, and that he had been listening to her murmured apology to Gemma.

He was frowning now as he studied her, no doubt wondering why on earth he had ever felt the slightest degree of physical desire for her, Holly reflected miserably. She only had to compare herself with Candice...to see the other woman's glowing air of vitality and confidence, to see herself, Holly, as Robert must be seeing her, her skin too pale, from tension and nervous stress, her body lacking Candice's voluptuous curves, her conversation lacking Candice's wit. And yet for all her envy she could not dislike the American, who was as charming to her fellow female guests as she was to the men.

Paul was obviously completely smitten with her, flirting so outrageously with her that Holly was amazed at Robert's forbearance, as he sat quietly watching Paul flirt with Candice without appearing in the least disturbed by it.

After dinner everyone returned to the drawing-room. Paul made an immediate bee-line for

Candice, who was the centre of a small group of admiring males.

Lost in her study of the American woman, Holly only realised that Robert was walking towards her when he said her name.

Immediately she froze, panic clawing at her. What was Robert going to say to her? Was he going to ask her not to betray him to Candice, not to reveal what had happened between them? Did he really think she was capable of that kind of cruelty?

Another step and he would be standing right next to her. Already her body was quivering with shock and despair; ignoring him completely, she turned on her heel and blundered out of the room.

Upstairs in one of the spare bedrooms she stared at her reflection in the mirror. Was it just the lights in the bedroom that made her skin look so pale and her eyes so full of misery?

She looked like someone with the cares of the world on her shoulders, a pale wraith of a woman who had lost a little too much weight a little too quickly.

Compared with Candice's obvious and abundant energy and health she looked like a convalescent. Holly gave a small, sharp shudder. If she had known about Candice before . . . She bit her lip, but she had not known and now it was too late to berate herself for allowing Robert to use her as a means of release from his physical desire for another woman.

He should be the one at whom she was directing her contempt, she tried to tell herself, but telling

herself that did nothing to remove the burden of
acute self-dislike from her shoulders.

It was late when she and Paul eventually left.
Once they were in the car, all Paul could talk about
was Candice. Holly bit her lip, too drained to
remind him that Candice was Robert's lover and
that Robert was his friend.

'You were very quiet this evening,' he commented just before he dropped her off. 'Robert
commented on it—asked me if you'd been over-
doing things.'

Holly turned her head away from him, unable to
make any response. Her eyes, she discovered, were
blurred with tears. She didn't know which was now
the stronger, her love for Robert or her hatred for
herself.

CHAPTER TEN

'Hi. I'm sorry to disturb you but Paul said it would be OK for me to come round. This sure is a lovely old place you have here.'

Holly tensed and then turned round. She had been working in the garden all morning and hadn't heard a car arrive, and the shock of hearing Candice's transatlantic accent had sent her whole body into a rigour of tension.

Now she moved deliberately, firmly digging the fork into the soil before she looked up into the face of her visitor, willing herself to appear calm and natural as she forced her tense face into a smile.

'How old is it, by the way?' Candice asked her as Holly joined her on the path.

'Fourteenth century,' Holly told her, trying to soften the curtness of her voice. It wasn't Candice's fault that Robert wanted her... loved her.

She was conscious of the sharp look Candice was giving her, her body tensing as the other woman said quietly, 'Look, if I've come at a bad time...'

She really must stop this, must get a grip on herself before Candice guessed.

Holly shook her head.

'No, no, of course you haven't. I was just about to stop anyway and have a cup of coffee.'

She moved off down the path, careful not to get too close to Candice with her muddy boots and jeans, opened the kitchen door, and ushered her inside before removing her wellingtons in the porch.

'Say, this kitchen is wonderful,' she heard Candice saying as she walked through to join her.

'It reminds me a little of my grandparents' place in New York State. It's kind of homey and welcoming, if you know what I mean. Whenever I get a little city sickness coming over me, I hightail it out of New York and go stay with them for a time.'

Holly washed her hands and then started making the coffee, taking some fresh beans from the sealed jar and putting them in the grinder. The noise it made rendered conversation impossible, but she couldn't keep it going forever, she recognised guiltily.

She had no idea why on earth Candice had come to see her, but her stomach was churning frantically, and, although from her demeanour it seemed impossible that the other woman was here to challenge her about her behaviour with Robert, Holly was still sickly conscious of her own burden of guilt.

Her hands were still shaking a little ten minutes later when she poured the coffee.

If she was aware of Holly's agitation Candice wasn't showing it. She picked up her coffee-mug, wrapping her elegant, manicured fingers around it, exclaiming, 'This smells real good!'

She took a sip, savouring it, and then put down her mug.

'I guess you already know what I'm here to talk about,' she said quietly.

Holly's heart leapt against her chest wall. She sat down clumsily, colour sweeping her face from her forehead to her jaw.

'I've known Robert for a long time,' Candice continued evenly. 'I guess you could say I must be about the first real friend he made in New York. Then I was new to the city myself, a bit young and raw, and he was a man totally outside my experience and I guess you could say that I fell a little in love with him right there and then.'

Holly felt sick. Please God, don't let this be happening, she prayed frantically, but it was and there was nothing she could do to stop it, nothing at all.

'I . . . I'm not sure what all this has to do with me,' Holly said thickly, her throat almost choked with guilt and despair.

Had Candice guessed? Has she somehow betrayed the truth?

There was a brief silence and when Holly could bring herself to look across the table at her unexpected guest she discovered that Candice was looking back at her gravely.

'One night Robert took me to a party—or rather I took him,' Candice corrected herself, ignoring Holly's outburst. 'It was in a loft . . . an artist friend of mine. There wasn't much food, but plenty to drink. It was the first and the only time I've ever seen Robert drunk.

'I took him home with me to my apartment . . .' She paused, while Holly tensed, every nerve-ending in her body screaming denial of what she knew she was about to hear. No matter how much she might deserve it, she could not endure this kind of torture.

She could not endure hearing the story of Candice's relationship with Robert...she could not endure knowing the reality of their relationship, their love-affair.

'We started talking,' Candice paused, her mouth twisting wryly. 'I pretty soon learned just how hopeless my case was when Robert started to tell me about a girl he'd left behind him in England...a girl he plainly still loved. Once he had started talking about her, it seemed that he couldn't stop. I heard all about her—her beauty, her intelligence...all about how badly he'd treated her and how much he regretted it, and I knew then even before Robert himself said the words that he'd go on loving her for the rest of his life.

'I was lucky. I was young enough and tough enough to find someone else to love. Robert wasn't so lucky...

'I asked Robert why, if he loved her so much, he didn't go back to her. He told me that it was too late and that he'd hurt her too badly...that she'd never forgive him and that he didn't deserve either her forgiveness or her love.

'Six months ago, when he told me he was coming back to England, I asked him if he still loved her...that girl. He said yes. I asked him what, if anything, he intended to do about it. He said he'd reached a point in his life where he had to make one last attempt to reach out to her...to tell her how he felt and to see if there was any chance that they could start again, and that if the answer was no, then he knew that he would have to accept that he must spend the rest of his life alone because he would never love anyone else, and he was not going to ask another woman to accept a very poor second best.

'I'd stopped loving him as a man years ago, but I still love him as a friend ... and it's as his friend that I'm here today, Holly, to ask you as another woman why, when it's so patently obvious how the two of you feel about one another, you're still apart.'

Holly couldn't help it. She burst into tears.

Instantly Candice took hold of her, holding her much as her own mother might have done, while Holly protested tearfully that she was muddy and dirty and that she would ruin the expensive cream cashmere outfit that Candice was wearing, and yet totally unable to draw away from her, to deny herself the wholly female pleasure of sharing her emotions with another woman and knowing that they would be instantly and unquestioningly understood.

'So I was right!' Candice exclaimed triumphantly when Holly finally drew away from her and blew her nose. 'I knew the moment I saw you the other night that you loved him, while poor Robert ... well, he could hardly drag his attention away from you all night. So then why, *why* are the two of you still apart?'

Holly shook her head.

'I thought he didn't love me. When he left me he told me that I'd never mattered to him, that he'd never really loved me, that it was only physical ... that it was only sex. I tried to get over him, to put him out of my heart. I told myself it was because of the pain he'd caused me that I was so wary with other men, refusing to admit that it was because I still loved him ... because they could never touch my heart, my emotions the way he had done. I had the business, my home ... I told myself that I was content, and then he came back, and I knew almost instantly that I still loved him ...

'I thought that you and he were lovers,' Holly told Candice shakily. 'I felt so guilty about that, especially——' She stopped, her face flaming.

Candice was watching her, but tactfully said nothing, other than a firm, 'Never. And in fact I happen to know that there hasn't been *anyone* else for Robert. Not that scores of women haven't tried. He's an extremely attractive man ... the kind of man who in New York ...' She gave a faint shrug and then said quietly, 'He's a man of honour, Holly ... a man whose love is far, far stronger than any mere physical sexual appetite.'

Holly's face flushed again as she remembered how in her heart she had accused Robert of merely wanting her for sex ... of using her to satiate his physical desire. How wrong she had been. How unfairly she had judged him.

'But if, as you say, he loves me, why did he never say anything? Why did he never get in touch with me? Why?'

'Aren't those questions you should ask him, and not me?' Candice asked her drily. 'I've done my bit, played my part as fairy godmother. Honestly, when I saw the two of you at that dinner party, I could have knocked your heads together. It was so glaringly obvious how you felt about one another.

Every time you so much as looked at each other, the whole room virtually vibrated with the sexual tension between you. You do love him, don't you, Holly?'

What was the point in denying it?

Holly nodded her head.

'Yes. Always and forever...'

Candice gave her a satisfied smile and then said, 'Well, why don't you tell *him* that?'

'Me, tell *him*?' Holly stared at her, her eyes rounding. What if Candice was wrong? What if Robert didn't give a damn about her after all? She could just imagine the scene...her pouring her heart out to him, laying her love at his feet...his shocked distaste, his embarrassment...his rejection.

'Why not?' Candice asked evenly. 'Believe me, in your shoes I wouldn't even hesitate.'

She glanced at her watch.

'Look, I've got to go. I've got a dinner date. No, not with Robert,' she said, grinning a little. 'As far as I know, he's spending the evening quietly on his own—no doubt daydreaming about the woman he loves. No, my date for the evening is your brother... Now, tell me, Holly, one woman to another... How do you rate my chances of persuading him that his freedom isn't such a wonderful thing after all? Come to that, how do you feel about having an American sister-in-law?'

After she got her breath back, Holly laughed.

'If that sister-in-law is going to be you, I think it's a great idea,' she told her, and added, 'Try reminding Paul that he's not getting any younger and that if I marry first I'll be providing the company with a clutch of potential new executives, while all he'll be doing is playing bachelor uncle.'

Holly walked with Candice to her car. They exchanged brief hugs and as she released her Candice said quietly to Holly, 'Go to him, Holly. Every word I've told you is the truth. Perhaps in fairy-tales it's always the man who makes the moves, while the woman waits demurely for him to do so, but men aren't gods, they're only human. Sometimes they suffer from all the doubts, all the fears, all the dreads that we women experience. Sometimes they too need the comfort of knowing that they're wanted...chosen.'

An hour later, as she stared out of her bedroom window, Holly tried to remind herself of everything that Candice had said, but her courage was quickly draining away. What if Candice was wrong? What if she had misunderstood? What if...?

But what if Robert did love her? What if, when he had made love to her, it had been because of that love, a love which she had not even allowed him time to express, so desperate was her need to maintain her own pride?

Before she could change her mind, she snatched up her jacket and hurried downstairs and out to the car.

It was still light when she reached the cottage, no lights in evidence inside it, no sign outside of Robert's car. Cravenly she told herself that he must have gone out, but nevertheless she made herself approach the door and lift the knocker.

She waited two and then three minutes before finally accepting that the house was empty. She had just turned away and was about to walk back down the steps when the door suddenly opened and Robert was standing there.

It was obvious that he had just got out of the bath or shower. He had pulled on a towelling robe but she could see the beads of moisture streaming down his bare legs.

'Holly?' The incredulity in his voice made her stomach churn. She longed to simply close her eyes and disappear. What on earth was she doing here? she wondered in angry despair. She had been a fool to ever have listened to Candice, to ever have believed ...

'I...'

'Look, you'd better come in,' Robert was saying, and before she could stop him he came towards her as though he was going to physically propel her inside if she tried to walk away.

Shakily she followed him inside.

'I was just having a shower,' he told her unnecessarily. 'I've been trying to dig over the vegetable patch. I had a couple of men in the other week clearing the worst of the rubbish from it. It's a long time since I've done any digging, and my shoulders feel as though they're on fire.'

He grimaced a little, flexing his muscles as he spoke, his conversation so mundane and ordinary that Holly found that she was able to relax.

'Look, if you can hang on for ten minutes or so, I'll go back upstairs and get dried and dressed and then——'

'No.' Holly knew that if she had to wait downstairs for two minutes, never mind ten, she would lose her courage and leave. 'No, I have to talk to you now,' she told him desperately, watching the way he frowned and then dragging her gaze from his face and unwittingly focusing it on the bare V of damp flesh exposed by his carelessly fastened robe.

The effect of that was even more disturbing than looking at his face had been. She felt weak and light-headed with the enormity of what she was contemplating doing, her stomach still churning with the powerful effect of a cement-mixer.

Initially she had planned to ask him delicately if it was true that he still cared for her, but suddenly she knew that she could not do that...that she could not ask him a question which she suspected he would immediately reject.

He must have become aware of her tension, because he suddenly said quietly and anxiously, 'Holly, what is it? What's wrong? Is it Paul...has something happened?'

Immediately she shook her head.

'No, no it's not Paul.' She took a deep breath and before she knew what she was doing she heard herself saying urgently, 'Robert, I...I love you. I've always loved you and I always will love you and when...when we made love...it wasn't because I wanted to forget you, nor was it because I wanted to be free to love someone else...I—there's never been anyone else for me like that...no other man, no other lover. I...I just couldn't. Not when——' She swallowed, her voice trailing away, her skin on fire as she suddenly realised what she was saying, what she was doing.

When she looked up into Robert's face it was like a mask. She started to tremble violently, knowing sickly that Candice had been wrong, that the whole thing had been a dreadful mistake, that Robert *didn't* love her after all. He looked like a man who had been turned to stone...and no wonder. She must have embarrassed him hideously. He must have no idea of what on earth he could say to her.

She made a small sound somewhere between a gulp and a sob and spun round on her heel, heading desperately for the door, but Robert reached it before her, barring her way, causing her to run full tilt into him.

As his arms closed around her, his fingers bit into her skin as he shook her, demanding rawly, 'Just what the hell are you trying to do to me? You tell me you love me and then you try to walk away from me. My God, Holly, just how much torment do you think I can stand? Is it true?' he demanded roughly. 'Can it really be true, or am I dreaming? How can you love me after what I did to you, after the way I treated you...hurt you?'

He was groaning the words against her mouth, in between kisses that made her lips tremble and then part, so that the sounds of his words were lost as she twisted her arms around his neck and buried her fingers in his hair, clinging unashamedly to him.

'Holly, Holly...I can't believe any of this is happening. I can't believe what I'm hearing. Is it really true...or am I just imagining it? You love me? I don't deserve this. I don't deserve you. When...what...?' He kissed her again as she made a small impatient sound deep in her throat, holding her against him so that her clothes grew damp from the intimate contact with his body.

'I can't believe this is happening,' Robert repeated, whispering the words against her mouth as his hands moulded her body. Against her ear he groaned, 'I've got to go upstairs and get dressed. We need to talk and if I stay here with you like this...'

He didn't need to say any more. She could feel the arousal of his body and knew that her own was already reacting to it and, much as she longed to make love with him, there were things that had to be said, explanations to be given.

As he slowly released her, Robert groaned again. 'I can't bear to let you out of my sight in case you disappear... Come upstairs with me. I'll get dressed in the bathroom. But at least I'll be able to talk to you.'

Holly made to move away from him, but he wouldn't let her, keeping hold of her as they walked upstairs together. The bathroom door was open, the air smelling of warmth and soap.

As he disappeared inside it, a betraying ache seized her lower body. She closed her eyes and then immediately opened them again as she was tormented by mental images of his naked body.

She shivered as she stood outside the bathroom, trying not to listen to the sounds of him drying himself and then starting to get dressed, trying desperately not to visualise his naked body.

'Holly, are you still there?' Robert demanded from behind the half-closed door. She nodded her head, and then froze as the door was flung open and she saw the look of panic and despair on his face.

With a small sob she ran to him. He dropped the shirt he was holding and wrapped his arms around her, whispering against her hair, 'I thought you'd gone. Oh, God, Holly, I can't bear this...can't bear being without you. Not now...'

He kissed her again. Her hands were pressed flat against his chest, her body aching with the torment of being so close to him. Both of them knew what was going to happen, and when he picked her up and carried her into his bedroom Holly reached out and touched his face with trembling fingers, as anxious to reassure herself that he was real as he was her.

They made love fiercely and quickly, and then lay together in the moist heat of the rumpled bed, Holly still trembling in the aftermath of their passion.

'I've thought of you like this so often,' Robert told her. 'Wanted you like this...ached for you like this. I should never have left you, Holly...never.'

'You said you didn't love me.' The words were painfully hard for her to say. They made her throat ache and her eyes burn.

'I lied to you. I've always loved you.'

'Then why?'

Quietly he explained, telling her about his parents' relationship, his own fears and doubts...his realisation that he had been wrong.

'But you could have got in touch with me.'

He shook his head.

'I thought you wouldn't want me back...that it was too late. I told myself that I had no right to try and disrupt your life, and then I started reading about you in the financial Press. I learned that you weren't married and I began to hope...to plan.

'I thought the other night that I had a chance, that it might be possible for me to realise all my dreams and then you told me that you didn't want me...that I meant nothing to you.

'What made you change your mind, Holly? What made you come to see me today?'

'Candice came to see me,' she told him. 'She told me that you loved me, that you'd always loved me. She told me that in my shoes, loving you the way she knew I did love you, she would find the courage to admit that love; and so that's what I decided to do.' She looked at him and told him huskily, 'I love you, Robert.'

Her startled eyes registered the sudden sheen of tears in his eyes, her fingertip gently touching the moisture on his skin, her lips tenderly absorbing it as she held him in her arms and wept inwardly for the pain they had both known.

Later they made love again, slowly and tenderly, savouring each caress, silently reaffirming their love for one another, joyously making a shared unspoken vow that they would never again risk the precious gift of that love.

Later still they had supper together, quietly planning their wedding, their lives... The company would always be important to her, Holly told him, and he accepted that this would be so, but she added that she would be quite happy to take a more low-key role in it, especially once they had children. It had always been the use of nature's gifts which had interested and motivated her rather than the high-pressure world of marketing and big business and she was more than happy to leave that aspect of the business to Paul.

They would live in the farmhouse, they decided, until the Hall was fit for occupation.

Just before she finally fell asleep in his arms, Robert whispered teasingly in her ear, 'You realise, don't you, that now you'll have to reorganise the garden for me?'

Holly smiled and snuggled up against him, whispering in response, 'The things some men will do just to get out of a bit of digging.'

They were both laughing as they kissed one final time before sleep claimed them.

If you are looking for more titles by

PENNY JORDAN

Don't miss these fabulous stories by one of
Harlequin's most renowned authors:

Harlequin Presents®

MILLION DOLLAR SWEEPSTAKES (III)

No purchase necessary. To enter the sweepstakes and receive the Free Books and Surprise Gift, follow the directions published and complete and mail your "Win A Fortune" Game Card. If not taking advantage of the book and gift offer or if the "Win A Fortune" Game Card is missing, you may enter by hand-printing your name and address on a 3" X 5" card and mailing it (limit: one entry per envelope) via First Class Mail to: Million Dollar Sweepstakes (III) "Win A Fortune" Game, P.O. Box 1867, Buffalo, NY 14269-1867, or Million Dollar Sweepstakes (III) "Win A Fortune" Game, P.O. Box 609, Fort Erie, Ontario L2A 5X3. When your entry is received, you will be assigned sweepstakes numbers. To be eligible entries must be received no later than March 31, 1996. No liability is assumed for printing errors or lost, late or misdirected entries. Odds of winning are determined by the number of eligible entries distributed and received.

Sweepstakes open to residents of the U.S. (except Puerto Rico), Canada, Europe and Taiwan who are 18 years of age or older. All applicable laws and regulations apply. Sweepstakes offer void wherever prohibited by law. Values of all prizes are in U.S. currency. This sweepstakes is presented by Torstar Corp, its subsidiaries and affiliates, in conjunction with book, merchandise and/or product offerings. For a copy of the official rules governing this sweepstakes offer, send a self-addressed, stamped envelope (WA residents need not affix return postage) to: MILLION DOLLAR SWEEPSTAKES (III) Rules, P.O. Box 4573, Blair, NE 68009, USA.

SWP-H895

As a *Privileged Woman,*
you'll be entitled to all these *Free Benefits.* And *Free Gifts,* too.

To thank you for buying our books, we've designed an exclusive FREE program called *PAGES & PRIVILEGES™*. You can enroll with just one Proof of Purchase, and get the kind of luxuries that, until now, you could only read about.

*B*IG HOTEL DISCOUNTS

A privileged woman stays in the finest hotels. And so can you—at up to 60% off! Imagine standing in a hotel check-in line and watching as the guest in front of you pays $150 for the same room that's only costing you $60. Your *Pages & Privileges* discounts are good at Sheraton, Marriott, Best Western, Hyatt and thousands of other fine hotels all over the U.S., Canada and Europe.

*F*REE DISCOUNT TRAVEL SERVICE

A privileged woman is always jetting to romantic places. When you fly, just make one phone call for the lowest published airfare at time of booking—or double the difference back! PLUS—

you'll get a $25 voucher to use the first time you book a flight AND 5% cash back on every ticket you buy thereafter through the travel service!

HP-PP4A

ℱREE GIFTS!

A privileged woman is always getting wonderful gifts.
Luxuriate in rich fragrances that will stir your senses (and his). This gift-boxed assortment of fine perfumes includes three popular scents, each in a beautiful designer bottle. <u>Truly Lace</u>...This luxurious fragrance unveils your sensuous side. <u>L'Effleur</u>...discover the romance of the Victorian era with this soft floral. <u>Muguet des bois</u>...a single note floral of singular beauty.

YOURS FREE!

$50 VALUE

ℱREE INSIDER TIPS LETTER

A privileged woman is always informed. And you'll be, too, with our free letter full of fascinating information and sneak previews of upcoming books.

ℳORE GREAT GIFTS & BENEFITS TO COME

A privileged woman always has a lot to look forward to. And so will you. You get all these wonderful FREE gifts and benefits now with only one purchase...and there are no additional purchases required. However, each additional retail purchase of Harlequin and Silhouette books brings you a step closer to even more great FREE benefits like half-price movie tickets... and even more FREE gifts.

L'Effleur...This basketful of romance lets you discover L'Effleur from head to toe, heart to home.

Truly Lace...
A basket spun with the sensuous luxuries of Truly Lace, including Dusting Powder in a reusable satin and lace covered box.

Complete the Enrollment Form in the front of this book and mail it with this Proof of Purchase.

PROOF OF PURCHASE
Offer expires October 31, 1996

HP-PP4